King Richard III and Anne Neville,
Their Love Story

Sylvia Charlewood

SpringwoodHouse Publishing.

King Richard III And Queen Anne Neville.
Their Love Story

Sylvia Charlewood

First Published by Springwoodhouse Publishing
12. Hillands Drive, Cheltenham.GL53 9EU

Dedication.

This book is dedicated to King Richard and Queen Anne, and to all those who work to preserve their Memory.

Loyauté Me Lie

Loyalty binds me to my God,
Now, and when I am under sod.

Loyalty binds me to my wife,
She is more precious than my life.

Loyalty binds me to our love,
A very gift from heaven above.

Loyalty binds me to our son,
He whose life has just begun.

Loyalty binds me to my friends
With whom I share all common ends

Loyalty binds me to this land.
Which I defend with heart and hand.

Loyalty binds me to my crown
That I'll not cravenly lay down!
And still, Loyalty binds me.

Sylvia Charlewood. 2015.

King Richard III and Anne Neville; The Love Story.

Introduction.

Nobody knows what Richard Plantagenet and Anne Neville said to each other, except for the words of their marriage service which would have been either in Latin, or Norman French or English. I would guess the vows would be made in English.

I have used the events of King Richard III's life and reign as a frame for my story: a story that obviously has to be imaginary.

I have taken the liberty of making the duke of Buckingham arrive at Northampton, and invite Lord Rivers to supper in advance of Richard of Gloucester. I know that this is not correct historically, but it helps my story.

All that we know for certain about Richard and Anne's private life together is that Richard married Anne Neville after she was widowed, following her extremely short marriage to the son of Margaret of Anjou and King Henry VI. We do know that Richard's older brother George, Duke of Clarence, had claimed so much of Anne's patrimony that Richard married her when she was more or less penniless. It is also known that Richard and Anne would have met while he was in her father's household, and that they were related to each other.

Because royal marriages were made for political or financial reasons and Richard's marriage to Anne did not follow any of these criteria, and because they did know each other in their young days, I believe that we may assume that Richard married Anne for love. Certainly what we know of their lives and of his reaction to her death bears out this supposition. Therefore I have written how their lives might have been. The dialogues are of course all imagined. But they might have happened something along these lines.

I have tried to present the Richard that I have come to know from the many books that I have read about him and his deeds and letters. Many people still see him as a child-killer. I believe this is so unlike anything that Richard ever did or said or expressed an opinion about, that it cannot be true. Here was a man who was full of a sense of Justice, and justice for all people, not just 'the great and the good', a man who showed mercy to the widows and children of those who rebelled against him. A man who actually did more for his country than most of those who came after him, and a man to whom we owe a great many debts to this day.

Shakespeare wrote 'The good men do is oft interred with their bones' and that is certainly true of King Richard III.

This book is mainly a romantic story, not a history. Perhaps it is not even an historical novel. Just a love story! I hope that you enjoy it for what it is – simply my own vision of the love between King Richard III and his Queen, Anne.

I would like to thank my family for their patience and forbearance, and especially my son for his inestimable help in publishing this book. S. A. Charlewood.

Index   Page

Chapter 1.

The Prince and the Beggar

It wasn't much just a few pence for a beggar sitting at the roadside, his back to a wall but it changed many lives. The man who gave the coins that had been jingling in his purse would not miss them for he was wealthy although young and they meant little to him, a small act of charity that he could well afford. Not that he looked richly dressed. The soft leather boots which were the first thing the beggar saw, were patched and none too clean. The cloak that hung down to the top of the boots was travel-stained and seemed threadbare. Not a man, one would think, to give away coins. In fact he did not seem like a man to have coins to give away. Yet his appearance was deceptive.

The hand held down to drop the coins into the beggar's hand was white, slender and well kept although strong and a little calloused. The voice that accompanied the gift with a kindly greeting was refined and cultured, not a voice to be associated with worn boots and shabby cloaks. Glancing up to thank his benefactor the man saw a rather tanned face framed in light golden-brown hair and deep set blue eyes beneath a slightly wrinkled brow. It was not wrinkled by age but rather by puzzlement. The eyes were frank and friendly and twinkled, inviting trust. The curved mouth smiled encouragingly. The man sitting by the wall smiled in return and confidently spoke his thanks.

The two men weighed each other up for few moments then 'Come with me to the inn and join me in a meal.' The seated man was taken aback for charity did not usually run this far.

But reassured by those frank and friendly eyes he got to his feet and gathered his scrip his stick and his rather tattered cloak. He was a little taller than the blue eyed man and older, for this was a youth still although he carried himself with certainty and confidence. The older man was slightly bent and rather thin and was still at a loss, but he had the air of one who had seen far better days. 'Why do you ask me to join you?' he asked 'Not many folk take notice of me let alone invite my company to eat with them!' The young man laughed and held out his hand saying 'Do you not want dinner? It is past the hour. I am hungry and I want company. That is all. Are you too proud to accept my friend?' 'No. Not at all' replied the man 'I too am hungry and will right gladly join you if you can abide my tatterdemalion looks!' 'Come then' said his benefactor 'let us go in and eat at this inn, their venison pasty is good! While we eat we can become better acquainted.' They went together into the 'White Hart' the nearby Inn.

The inn was less crowded than usual it being past the normal hour for dinner and the innkeeper quickly found a place for them near to the great fire place where some large logs burned fitfully.

The serving girl was not busy now and so was able to give them good attention. She gave a quick bob saying 'Well, sirs, and what shall I fetch for you?' 'Two tankards of good ale and two trenchers of game pie if you please my lass.' said the blue eyed young man. He turned to his companion 'Now let us be seated my friend and we will warm ourselves for it still gets chilly even though it is already May!' The older man stirred the logs to flame and then seated himself on a stool by the hearth. He asked 'Why do you take an interest in me?' The young man dropped his voice 'Can you be secret?' he enquired. 'Silent as the grave so that you ask me to do no ill.' was the reply. 'Why then here it is,' said the young man 'I am looking for a servitor someone whom I can trust and one who has no ties to hold him in one place. You are an honest man as I can see in your face and I see too that you belong to no one place and are a stranger here as I am myself and you are a beggar so you will be in need although you do beg with some dignity.'

'I am no beggar!' The older man was angry 'I am well born I but I am a younger son and must make a living where I can. I work, master, I do not beg!' He was clearly much angered by being called a beggar 'I am a traveller as are you' he said 'and I was resting against that wall for shelter from the wind and wondering where I could find work. I am no beggar!' He had sprung up from his seat.

His companion smiled his apology 'I see well now that you are not and I regret that I should have so mistaken you. Please be seated! Tell me your name, friend, and your story. Then I will share mine with you.'

The other man calmed himself and he said 'I am as I have said a younger son. My father is dead and I had no wish to hang on the coat-tails of my older brother in whose house I would be a mere servant ordered about where before I had given orders. So I left. I have travelled far and done much work but it was always honest work. I was raised a gentleman in a gentleman's house and I have been trained as an esquire. I can fight but I choose not to use my sword and I am an honest man.' 'Very well' said the blue eyed man 'let me know your name and please, do be seated!'

The man did as he was asked and seated once more he said 'My name is Luke for I was born on that Saint's feast day'. 'Well then, Luke, I need a man who will serve me. My name is Richard and my lands are in the North Country. My man-servant was homesick, newly wed as he was, so I let him go home to York and his pretty wife. I need a man-servant. You are honest of that I am certain for I can read the characters of men. And you need employ, so will you be my man? I can assure you that I too am honest. I am no cut-purse or outlaw but a man of property and responsibility who has a difficult task to perform. Will you help me?' Luke looked carefully into the frank blue eyes and said 'I see, Master, that you are indeed an honest man and being master-less and needing employment I will be your man-servant and will do my duty to you well and honestly!' His companion held out his hand 'Let us then be of one accord' he said and he and Luke shook hands.

The serving girl brought ale and hot food. The young man motioned Luke to the chair next to his own at the table 'Let us eat and while we enjoy this good pasty, I know it is good for I had some this morning! Tell me of your travels'. Luke told him 'I was born on my father's small manor near to Leicester. As he grew older and a little infirm I helped him to run the estate but he when died and my older brother came back to the manor which he had by right inherited, I found it impossible to remain there. So I have taken whatever employment I could find. I was bred up a gentleman, master, I can read and write I speak French and Italian I understand how to cast up figures and attend to account books and I can read and understand Latin although I do not write it. I was also trained in arms but having seen that great fight that was fought at Towton I never wish to see another! I have no wife and no sister and my mother is dead as is my father. I will not take the grudging scraps offered by my brother and become a servant in my own home. I have worked at many trades but never have I done dishonestly to any one. And there you have it master.' He took a deep draught from his flagon of ale and was silent.

The younger man waited for a few moments then he explained. 'I must go to London, Luke, to find a lady who has been abducted. I have an idea of where she may be but to find her and bring her away will be difficult and I think I cannot do it alone. I do not need your sword nor will I ask that of you for I know of Towton fight, but I need a man who can assist me in other ways. One who can be as you said you were unnoticed. I am in haste or my love is lost and her inheritance eaten up.' 'Then I am your man.' said Luke. 'I am glad of that for I have much to do and little time to lose.' said his benefactor.

'Tell me, master, how I should address you?' asked Luke. 'Why, man, by my name. I am called Richard!' replied his new master. 'Then I shall call you Master Richard for that seems most proper to me. Which chamber have you taken here? I will go and make it ready and attend to your clothing.' Luke was already on his feet 'It shall be as you wish' said the young man 'We will both go and I will show you what I want you to do. But I believe I must first find you a change of linen for I see that my shirts will not suit you. You have an inch or two more than I!' said Master Richard and they went up the staircase of the inn to his lodging.

The White Hart Inn was the largest and most prosperous in the town and Master Richard had taken the best chamber there. The walls were painted with patterns of flowers and leaves and these patterns were repeated in the tapestry that hung round the bed and over the doors. The windows were glazed and had tapestry hangings to keep out the cold and cover the shutters. As well as the bed there was an oaken table a couple of stools and an armed chair. Two great wooden coffers stood against the wall and there was also a prie-dieu on which Luke noticed was an open book. The privy was hidden by a tapestry and there were perches for clothes. In the great hearth a fire was ready laid. Rushes and sprigs of rosemary were strewn over the floor and a fine carpet was laid over the table. It seemed that Richard had much baggage for two large travelling trunks stood against another wall and were seemingly unopened. On a stand were a jug and basin for washing and clean linen towels were piled on the shelf beneath; it was in fact as fine a room as any man could wish for in an inn and was costly – as Luke remarked.

'I live simply' said Richard, 'but I see no sense in stinting on comfort though I wish for no great display. Fresh linen, hot water, good food and a decent bed are all I require. Take this,' he said handing Luke a heavy purse 'go into the town and supply yourself with enough body linen and with at least two changes of clothes two pairs of boots and another for riding. You also need a warm frieze cloth cloak and riding gloves. Then you may go and study my horse. The ostler will point her out to you. Find one to match her and buy it. Then come back to me here. He threw himself down on the bed and immediately fell asleep before the astonished Luke could leave the chamber. In the town Luke quickly found all the things he needed so that his commissions were soon carried out. Having bestowed his purchases safely he went to the inn stables to ask after the horse. His was amazed when he saw her for she was a magnificent grey with a beautiful tail and mane. Elegantly built, she was never the less strong enough to carry any man and she had a kind eye, bright, intelligent and friendly. He had never seen anything like this animal and the ostler told him 'She's mostly of Arab blood her line must have come home with some crusader. She's fleet of foot as a fairy. Tame and tough she is. You'll not find another like this!' Luke could not match her but he found a good grey gelding. He would never outrun the mare but he was a good horse and Luke bargained carefully for him, and got him at a fair price.

Returning to the great chamber Luke put away his bundles lit tapers and kindled the fire. The light woke his master who yawned and stretched and rubbed his eyes like a child. 'Well how do you, Luke, my friend?' he enquired. Luke returned the purse still full with unspent money and carefully accounted for every coin he had spent, each purchase he had made and its cost. 'Why man!' exclaimed an astonished Richard 'if you continue in this way I shall be a richer man come Yuletide!' And he pushed the purse back into Luke's hand. 'Keep it' he said 'for you will need money and you must have your wages.' 'That I cannot accept for there is enough money in this purse to buy two manors!' 'Why then do you buy them! or else spend what you will on whatever you will. But not yet' laughed his master. 'I have need of you still. That is your purse Luke and I will not take it back!' At length and after much argument the man agreed to keep the purse and concealed it in a place of safety. He wondered greatly what sort of man he had pledged himself to serve but his musings were interrupted by a tap on the door.

The maidservant was there with a steaming dish and a flask of wine for their supper.

Chapter 2.

A Friendship is Cemented

During their meal Richard said 'You have begun well, Luke, tell me again where were you raised?' 'In my father's house, Master Richard; he had a small manor outside Leicester and though not a wealthy man he had us all taught first by his house-priest and then in gentlemen's houses. So I know how to serve you, Master Richard, and I was also taught to cast up numbers and look over accounts. My mother insisted on it for she thought that otherwise I might be cheated!' 'She did right to think of it' said his master 'there are too many, scholars of law especially, ready to dip their hands into other folk's purses! And I for one believe that all business should be done in plain English such as we all speak and that every man and every woman too should read and write and number! I would change many laws if I could. Your hand and eye will be of great use to me. I trust few lawyers! Now let us address ourselves more carefully to this fine supper – it is better eaten hot than cold!'

Supper was simple but delicious and ample as befitted the resident of the best room in the house. Only white bread was served with cheese, cold meats and good wine instead of ale and it was followed by a dish of fruits in season. Luke enjoyed it but still wondered what man he had agreed to serve.

When the meal was finished Richard stood up stretching himself and wincing very slightly. 'Come' he said, 'let us go out into the town and see what's to do!' The two men wrapped their cloaks around them and went downstairs and out into the street. The town was quiet and there was no more than the sound of a drunken man who laughed then hiccupped and then wept to disturb the stillness. 'All's quiet here.' said Master Richard.

'Nay, now don't you be saying that!' said a voice and turning Richard saw an old man sitting on a low wall. 'Why should I not believe this to be a quiet and peaceful place?' he asked. The ancient replied 'Because we've had our rights took away from us that's why!' 'And who has taken away your rights? Who has done this?' Asked Richard angrily and the old man told a long and involved story of how someone had come to the town and demanded taxes from the townsmen and had collected them at knife point. He had gone from house to house carrying a lighted torch and threatening to fire the house if the householder refused to pay in cash or in kind. This, said the old man, had been done in the name of the king and the extortioners were expected to return after the next fair. 'Write all this down Luke' said Richard, 'we must always take note of what the people say and what they most need. In this case it seems that it is justice"! Write it down!' Luke wrote all that the aged man had told them. Richard asked the townsman how much he had had stolen from him and gave for the few pence mentioned, two silver coins. As he and Luke walked away the grandsire called down blessings on both their heads. Although they visited every nook and cranny and every house and tavern they heard no other such stories although some of the people did look frightened and hid when they saw 'foreigners'. 'You see now why I wear scuffed boots and an old cloak,' said Richard 'poor men usually hate the man just one rank above them even more heartily than they hate those in high office!' he laughed softly 'it's strange enough but true!'

And so they returned to the White Hart to drink a hot posset and retire to bed. Richard lay down in the great curtained bed and Luke closed the shutters over the windows and pulled the truckle bed from under Richard's bed. He pulled it right across the doorway so that no one could enter the room without waking him. He had learned well how to serve his master.

The next day dawned bright and a little warmer. Both men awoke early and Luke drew the drapes back from the shuttered windows and slid his truckle bed back under the great bed. Sunlight lit the dancing dust mites as it filtered round the edges of the shutters. Richard and Luke talked softly so as not to awaken other guests but from the clanks and bangs from below it was clear that many people were already up and working. Luke poured water from the jug into a small pan and blowing the embers of the fire into life he fed the sparks with fresh wood and placed the pan on the fire to warm so that Richard might wash and shave. Then he sharpened the razor from Richard's travelling bags and prepared to shave him.

This was an entirely new experience for both of them for Luke had never shaved anyone else before.

Luke was nervous, and he said as much but Richard kept very still and when it was finished he said 'Why look you, Luke, there is no looking-glass here so there is nothing for it but that I shave you my friend!' and he did. Both men found this amusing. Luke was impressed by the richness of the items in Richard's travelling chest and could not help wondering who his master truly was although a crest on something in the chest did strike a chord in his memory – but as he could not pin it down in his mind he soon forgot about it. As he stood cleaning the razors Richard said to him 'Luke you are many years younger than I believed you were now you are so clean shaven! I do believe that you are a mere stripling and probably even my junior by a few years!' Luke laughed. 'No, Master, I am older than you I believe. I have not thought much of my age of late but I think that I shall have some twenty nine summers come yuletide.' 'Why then you are my senior,' said his master 'but let us not quibble. I swear I have more white hairs than do you!' 'That is what comes from responsibility' said Luke 'but the white hairs show more in my dark head than in your lighter one! And I know now sir that you are nobly born for your chests and toilet articles all bear a crest and it is one that I recognize for I have seen it before.' 'That must be because they are my brother's' was the reply 'he lends me such things. Let us go and break our fast. What are a few grey hairs between us!' Luke agreed, forgot it and went with his master to enjoy a breakfast of small ale, bread and cheese laid out for them before the fire in the great room of the inn. While they ate in silence at first Luke had the opportunity to look hard at the young man for whom he had engaged to work. He felt certain that he had seen him long before the previous day. Years ago in fact, but he still could not quite recall the occasion. 'This is good bread' said Richard breaking some off the loaf 'eat well, my friend for I think today we should try that horse of yours. You say it is a good gelding?' 'Yes, Master Richard, so he is' replied the other 'he's a good mount but not as fine as your mare. Shall I go and fetch more suitable garments for you to ride in?' 'No just my cloak and these riding gloves are sufficient today. We will ride out a little way and try the gelding's paces. Are you ready?' Luke nodded assent over the lip of his ale mug wiped his fingers on the napkin and rose with Master Richard. They took their warm cloaks in spite of the sun knowing that in May the weather can change in a moment.

They went to the inn stables where everyone seemed very busy and found the elegant grey mare. An ostler appeared 'Fed and watered?' asked Master Richard 'Yes, sir and rubbed down and saddled up, and the gelding too – I did guess you'd be awanting to ride today!' The man seemed pleased when

Richard smiled his thanks and slipped him a coin. They led their horses out into the yard and mounted up.

It took only a few minutes to ride clear of the small town and to find a stretch of open heath-land where the horses could show their paces. Given their heads the two beasts raced off joyously but try as he might, the gelding could not best the grey mare! After a good gallop they slowed their mounts to a trot. 'Well done Luke' said his master 'you ride well and you have a good eye for horseflesh.' 'I was well tutored Master Richard but my gelding will never match that beautiful mare of yours! Why, she flies!' He was full of admiration for his master's mount. 'She is a great lady' said Richard, 'from a good lineage. There are few like her but there is one of her line also a grey, who I think may well do great things as a mount in warfare. I am watching his progress. But now that we are far from all ears we must talk privately' they brought their mounts to a halt. Richard swung down from the high saddle as did Luke and they tied the reins of their horses loosely to a sapling so that the beasts might graze. There was a fallen tree near by and on it they both sat.

'We must speak of many things and you must promise to be as close as you have been until now for my business is secret and concerns great things and great persons.' said Richard .'So I have surmised' rejoined Luke.

'England may seem to be at peace but it is not.' Richard said 'The King is pre-occupied and there are those who take what is not theirs to have. When he finds this out do you suppose the King will reward these thieves and rogues or will he, think you, rather punish such wrong doers?' The blue eyes under the slightly furrowed brow were not twinkling now. They looked concerned and determined and it seemed to Luke that they peered into his very soul. 'Master Richard' he said 'I believe that his Grace will be angered by such usage and will punish the perpetrators'. 'I am certain that he will and right quickly too! And I will help him!' said the other

'But first, Luke, we must travel to London. I am unwed my friend but the lady whom I love and whom I will wed has been abducted and hidden. My brother, my own older brother, wishes for her inheritance. He has married my Love's sister and as they are both their late father's heirs he plans to obtain all their lands and goods for himself. To that end he has spirited my love away and I must find her. I would marry her if she owned nothing but a shift but it is not justice, Luke, and I will not countenance what is not justice.' He slammed one fist into the other hand and seemed very angry but it was a cold anger. 'This is a careful man for his years', Luke thought, 'one who would not strike out without giving it great thought'.

There was silence for a few moments and Luke could hear the birds singing in the nearby copse and the insects busy in the grasses. Then the younger man spoke again. 'I have two brothers, Luke. I know it does not go well for you with your older brother, but my oldest brother is splendid and I serve him as well as I can. My other brother who is also older than I am is not trustworthy. See what he has done to my lady! Yet I love him and will not hurt him. But I must and will find her and I will marry her!'

Luke was silent for a few seconds then he said, very simply 'When shall we ride?' 'Tomorrow my friend.' said his master. 'Now let us go back to the inn for it is time to eat and to plan.' While they rode he questioned Luke about his training as an esquire and in whose house he had been placed for the training. Luke answered all the questions openly and truthfully but refused to discuss the battle of Towton in which he had taken part, although he did say that he had fought on the Yorkist side.

That seemed to please the younger man who clapped him on the back crying out that he had guessed all along that Luke was surely an honest fellow. 'And you, Master Richard, are the Duke of Gloucester.' said Luke 'I recall now where I have seen that badge of yours before!' 'I am he' said his master 'though I shall be glad if you will not divulge it until I tell you that you may.'

From that moment the two men were always together and there were no secrets between them. Not that there had ever been any tension in their relationship for they were both sensible and well educated men. On his side Richard of Gloucester found that Luke could sing and play the lute in addition to his other accomplishments. 'You are a man of parts' he told him 'and will grace my brother's Court when we reach it! I am sure that you will play havoc with the hearts of all the ladies!' 'Sir' said Luke 'I wish and have always wished to become a monk. But I will stay with you until you have found your lady and have wed her. I am your true man and always will be, but in time I wish to be God's man first!'

Chapter 3.

London and Baynard's Castle

Next day they left the White Hart. Luke had wondered how
they would carry those large travelling chests in Richard's
chamber, but he need not to have been concerned for a cart
with two great horses arrived with two hefty and silent men
who took the chests away by the usual road while Luke and his
master, mounted on their greys, went across country. The
younger man seemed to know the land well. 'I have hunted
over all this land here' he told Luke, 'so I know the quickest
way to London!'
They rode to the great house, Baynard's Castle not far from the
Tower of London where Richard's mother the Lady Cecily
lived. There they were greeted by about a dozen servants
running to meet them some were to take their horses and some
to escort them through the great gates. Inside Lady Cecily held
out open arms to enfold her son who having received her kiss
of welcome, knelt for her blessing.
'And this is Luke my servitor and my friend' said Richard
motioning Luke forward. 'You are welcome if you are truly a
friend to my son.' said the lady. 'I would die for him Lady' the
man said simply. 'Then you are indeed most welcome!' cried
lady Cecily 'Come in and take some wine for you must both be
tired although I know my son would never admit to it!' 'Yes,
Luke, come and drink with us' said Richard 'but I don't want
you ever to die for me! I want you alive and well with all your
faculties' and laughing he pushed Luke into a seat by the fire
and handed him a goblet of wine.

The two men told Lady Cecily of how they had met and what Richard had now to do. 'I believe that George has hidden the lady Anne' said Richard 'and I mean to find her as soon as I can. Mother I intend to marry her. George can have her inheritance if he needs it so badly. I love Anne and I will marry her even if she comes to me with only a shift!'

'I know my dear.' said the Lady 'And I can help. One of George's men has told me, for much gold, of course, where that poor girl is. I have been waiting for you for I cannot go there myself and trusted none of my people to fetch her safely back.' Her son was delighted 'Mother! Is this true?' his face which was usually so serious was lit like a lantern, 'Where must I go? Where is she?' 'My son' said Lady Cecily 'I speak truth so listen! You will find her in Southwark where George has lodged her in a house called "The Bird in the Hand" which I am sad to say is of ill repute. The house is in an alley, the third on the right hand behind the bishop's palace.' Richard's face darkened but she shook her head 'No, now, don't fear she has been put to work in the kitchens and has nothing to do with the men who frequent the house!'

Richard's face remained dark. 'George!' he cried, 'How could he do this! I will find her and then I will find George and I will.....' 'Stop! He is your brother and you must not seek reprisals!' his mother looked seriously concerned as she said 'Richard, George is covetous, greedy and foolish but I do not think he intended harm to Anne. I do believe that he would have told you of her whereabouts....' 'Yes but only when he had made certain of her inheritance!' thundered her son. 'Mother, Anne should not be there in that place and we all know it and we all know, also, what sort of man George is: untrustworthy and devious! Come Luke, we must go at once to find my lady!'

23

Chapter 4.

The Kitchen Maid.

Anne was trying to clean a particularly greasy pot with cold water in a dark cellar kitchen. The place was damp from the well in the corner and rats came running about even in the daytime, for it was never really light down there. They had stripped her of her fine clothes when she first arrived although she wondered how the grossly fat old woman who took her to the kitchen could possibly make use of them! Now she wore only a dirty shift which was wet from the washing of pots and greasy from them too. Tears came into her eyes as she recalled how first as the daughter of a great Earl and then as the Princess of Wales she had been beautifully attired and waited on by young ladies of her own age and rank. She was widowed now, for the odious young man to whom her father had married her was dead. Edward the Prince of Wales and son of Henry the Sixth had been killed in battle.

Anne was not sorry for this. She had not liked him because he was always boasting and always talking of killing people. Death in battle was probably what he would think proper for himself as a 'great warrior.' although she did not know of any battles in which he had taken part. They had never discussed anything. Indeed they had rarely spoken to each other. He had been stuck to the side of his mother and her advisers and had had no time for his bride. She was not sorry for that, either, because years ago she had given her heart to another.

Anne had been heart-broken when her father had informed her of this terrible marriage. She knew it was a political move on his part but that did not make it any better. Now both her husband and her father were dead and she was in this dreadful place, put here by her sister's husband. She thought of the young man whom she loved and tears welled up in her eyes so that she could no longer see the pot that she was trying to clean.

She stumbled over to the corner where behind the well, which smelled of foul water, was the bundle of old rags that the fat woman had given her to sleep on. 'There now, my pretty princess, you'll be snug on these!' the old hag had said. Anne laid herself down sobbing as she often did from tiredness, cold and hunger to say nothing of being dirty and lonely. She thought of her early life, surrounded by every comfort and every luxury, and of the people she loved. She thought of her mother who must be worried about where her younger daughter might be. And there was her sister Isabel. Anne wondered if Isabel's husband George had told his wife what he had done with her sister. And if Isabel did know would she tell anyone? And then what of Richard her great love? Anne sobbed harder because she loved Richard. She had loved him for as long as she could clearly remember. Now remembering that he loved her too, Anne stopped crying. Richard would not cry like a baby. Richard she knew would think and then he would plan. But she could plan nothing!

She did not even know where she was; it had been dark night when they had brought her to this place and she did not know who they were except that she thought she had glimpsed George's badge under one of their cloaks. What could she do? The fat old woman had never come to the kitchen again. There was only the old man who did the cooking somewhere upstairs in some other kitchen she supposed for although the room where she was incarcerated had a fire place it had never used while she had been there. She could smell cooking and once every day the silent old man brought her a plate of scraps. She had spoken to him once but he had shaken his head and pointed to his mouth and when she spoke again he had opened his mouth to show her he had no tongue. Horrified, she never spoke to him again but just tried to smile her thanks. She was now so thin that the dirty and ragged shift that they had given her fell in folds around her.

Thinking about the old man cooking upstairs she had an idea. Going over to the empty fire place she looked up the chimney for she knew that chimneys were built with footholds in the brick work so that sweepers could clean them. She also knew that if you looked up a chimney you could usually see the sky. She thought that if she climbed up inside this chimney she might get out onto the roof and escape. But there was no glimpse of sky up the chimney! It had been blocked part way up. She was disappointed and more tears came but she brushed them away and tried to think of some other way. Praying for help had not proved useful even though she had prayed to her name-sake saint as well as all the others she could think of. Her thoughts went to Richard again. She knew that he would have asked for her and that he would have seen Isabel and George and he must have asked where she was for she had been given into their keeping after her father had been killed in the great battle. Going back to her rag bed she tried to send her thoughts out to Richard.

'Oh, Richard, my Love, please make your brother tell you where I am. Please come and take me from this terrible place.' She gave up when her head began to ache from thinking and crying and went back to the wash bowl and the greasy pot that she found so hard to clean. While she had been preoccupied the pot had soaked a bit and she found cleaning it easier. She took that as a good omen. 'He will come and find me' she told herself. And she began to sing a little song it was just a catch that she had learned at Court. Almost at once the silent old man came down the stairs and made a sign that she should be silent. He drew a finger across his throat and shook a fist at her. Anne, terrified, was silent.

To summon up some comfort and courage Anne sat on the floor dirty and damp though it was, and recalled the sunny day when she had been sitting in the garden or her father's castle of Middleham in Yorkshire with her sister Isabel and their ladies and around them. She had been stringing daisies into a daisy chain while the others were deep in gossiping. A light tread beside her made her look up. Richard stood there. 'A fair day, my Lady!' he had said. 'It is a fair day my Lord Richard' she had responded. He had asked leave to sit with her and she had happily agreed. She was well chaperoned and this youth lived in her family as if he were her brother. They spoke of his knightly training and his new mount, a fine grey mare. He was four years her elder and busy learning how to be a knight.

He picked more daisies for her to add to her chain.

Then he solemnly took her hand. She did not mind for she was already in love with him and she was delighted when he told her 'My lady Anne, in a very little while now I shall be old enough to go to my lord you father and ask for your hand in marriage. Would you be happy to be my wife, dearest Anne?' his blue eyes were pleading. She threw her arms round his neck and told him that nothing in the world would make her happier than to be his wife! They had been mere children but they had recognized their love for each other and it had not faded away with time.

Then Anne remembered how not long after that and before Richard had had time to approach her father, she had been summoned before her parents to be told that she was to wed the

Prince of Wales son of King Henry VI and Queen Margaret. She had wept and protested but her father would not listen. The marriage was good for him he said and she must be an obedient child and do as she was bid and there was an end to the matter. So she had to marry the odious Edward and she was a most reluctant bride.

If Anne was sad Richard was broken-hearted. Worse, he had had to leave her father's household and could hardly speak when he took leave of her. His eyes, though, told her of his love and his misery at being parted from her.

Now she was in an even worse case than being married to the hateful Edward who so unlike the kindly, eccentric and saintly King Henry that she was inclined to believe the stories that he was not the King's true son but the child of Queen Margaret and some courtier with whom the queen had laid, so desperate for an heir was she. They whispered that when the King had been told that he had a son he said the baby must be the 'child of the Holy Ghost' since he 'knew nothing of it'!

Anne sent out more loving thoughts to Richard and prayed ceaselessly for him to come and find her. She thought of how after the battle at Tewkesbury when she, newly widowed, had been taken prisoner with Margaret of Anjou and the other Lancastrian ladies, Richard had found a way to speak with her very briefly just to reassure her of his love for her. His words had cheered her and given her courage.

Eventually having cleaned all the pots that had been brought to the cellar she went to her ragbag bed and slept.

Chapter 5.

The Rescue

Riding to Southwark late at night wrapped in hooded cloaks which hid their faces and with their horses' hooves wrapped in rags, Richard and Luke tied up their mounts at a decent inn and then proceeded on foot to look for the house called "The Bird in the Hand". Following Lady Cecily's instructions they soon found it. The inn where they had left their horses was not far away and they kept watch until the last light went out in the house where Richard fervently hoped that Anne was still being kept. He sent Luke who was unknown to any of Richard's brother George's servants, to look more closely at the house. It was only a very few minutes before Luke was beside him again having moved in almost total silence. 'There is but one entrance, Master, and no guards' he said 'there are no lights burning anywhere and I believe there is a cellar for I saw an aperture through which they can lower supplies but it is very small and I don't think we can get in that way.' Richard sighed softly. 'We must go in by the front door then.' he said. 'Stay here – no! Better still go back to the inn and fetch the horses and lead them to the end of this alley where we came in. Stay there with them until I come to you. I must go alone!'
Luke disappeared from the narrow alley and Richard walked very softly to the "Bird in the Hand". He walked to the front door, his soft, scuffed boots making little noise. He tried the door but it was fastened. So having thought for a moment he tapped on it softly. The door opened just a slight crack. Richard made out part of a man's face. 'I want a woman' said Richard making his usually quite light voice deep and growling. 'Now!'

29

he added. The door was pushed wider and the old man beckoned him in. At once Richard grabbed him by the throat to stop him making a noise. The old man's eyes popped wide open. 'The kitchen!' said Richard gruffly, and unspeaking the man pointed to a doorway. 'Open it' growled Richard. The old man was shaking and Richard felt guilty at scaring such a feeble old man but he was in a hurry and he did not want the whole house around his ears. The man shuffled along to the door fumbled uselessly, so Richard took a cord from under his cloak and tied the man's hands 'I will not hurt you if you stay quiet' he hissed. The man made a signal and Richard understood that he had no tongue.

Richard unbolted the door that the man had indicated and saw that it led to a cellar. He went down the stairs into the dark dank-smelling place. At the foot of the stairs he waited as his eyes became accustomed to the gloom; then he stepped forward. 'Anne' he said in a whisper. Something stirred at the far side of the dark space and he saw something pale coming towards him. 'Anne?' he whispered again, and there was a gasp. Anne could see by the faint light from the open doorway behind him and she recognized the outline of the young man she so dearly loved. He put the finger of his free hand to his lips lest she cry out. 'Come, my love, very softly! You are free but we must be quick and silent. Come, come to me!' Anne walked up the steps and she was trembling in every limb. Richard caught her in his free arm. Then he took her to the door. Whispering to the old man 'Wait and be still until we are well gone' he pressed a coin into the man's hand. Then he lifted the frail girl in his arms and hurried back to where Luke was ready waiting with the horses.

Richard wrapped his shivering lady in his cloak placed her before him on his horse and said to Luke 'Ride, my friend, ride to my mother and tell her that my lady is found' 'And you, Master?' asked Luke 'I will tell you when I return' said Richard.

Richard took the shortest way he knew to the where the Church of St Martin le Grand had been and where there was now a place of refuge. He told Anne that he was taking her to Sanctuary. When they arrived, he knocked loudly on the door. Someone opened it and he announced himself as the King's brother and showed the ring which he wore on his right hand. He demanded to see the warden and. Anne and Richard were ushered into a small room. Soon a rather pompous gentleman arrived in his bed-gown and obviously very much put out at being disturbed in the night. Richard said who he was and showed his badge of office and a large and heavy purse.

The fellow's demeanour changed at once. He rang a bell to summon a servant and told him 'Go and fetch my wife for she is needed here! And bring wine and cakes for this lady and gentleman!' Within a very few minutes his wife came bustling in. She was a plump good natured looking lady of a certain age, wrapped in a cloak over her night-rail. She took one look at Anne and said 'Poor child! Whatever has happened to you!' and took her in her arms. 'Do not ask this lady any questions, mistress, if you please!' said Richard and he took Anne gently from the woman's grasp and placed her on a seat before the remains of the fire which he kicked into life. 'Stay here my Lady, where you are safe, until I have spoken to my brother the King. This gentleman and his wife will care for you and I will visit often but you must rest, my love.'

Turning to the Warden and his wife Richard gave them clear instructions on how they should care for Lady Anne and keep her safe, saying that they must admit no-one to see her but himself or a man who would give his name as Luke. He took a cup of wine which he handed to Anne and then took one for himself. He drank her health and kissed her hand then he told the warden's wife to ensure that the lady was bathed, fed and dressed and put to bed in clean linen so that she might sleep. Then he left.

Anne thought she would awaken in the cellar again at any minute. She could hardly believe that her dreams had come true and that her dear Love had indeed rescued her! It was bliss to be put into a tub of warm water and washed by the clucking warden's wife then wrapped in warm linen towels dried, and given a clean shift of fine linen. Mistress Warden cooed 'Oh my pretty dear! How thin you are! Wherever you have been, you've not been cosseted! Now don't you worry your head my dear,' she cooed on 'I will look to your welfare and you may call me Mary for that's my given name. Now you only have to ask for whatever you want for that gallant young gentleman as brought you to us, he has given us good money enough for you to have the half of London!' 'I am very glad to be here, Mistress Mary' said Anne, trying not to weep for sheer relief 'I have been ill used but not violated and I am thankful to be warm and clean but I am so very tired!' 'Of course you are, my pretty, and you shall sleep soft! Are you able to walk up a pair of stairs to bed?' Anne smiled and it was the first time she had done so in a long time 'Yes, I can, I believe, walk up stairs' she said. So Mistress Mary guided her up to a pleasant room with a warm fire glowing in the hearth and heavy drapes over the casement and there she helped Anne into a real bed with clean white sheets, soft blankets and deep pillows. Anne was asleep before Mary could even wish her 'Good night, my poppet'.

Chapter 6,

At Baynard's Castle Again

Meanwhile Richard had returned to give his mother news. 'I feel inclined to meet out some punishment to my brother George!' He told her when he had explained how he had found Anne. 'Never fear my son, for George will one day pay for his mistakes I make no doubt of it.' Lady Cecily shook her head 'It will not do for my sons not to be at peace together for there has been too much conflict!' She looked sad and young Richard felt grieved for her. He hardly remembered his father or his oldest brother. But his mother's grief when she was widowed, her husband and her oldest son both killed, and she was left unprotected with her younger children to care for, was fresh in his memory. He clearly remembered standing at Ludlow market cross with his mother and his siblings, waiting to be taken prisoner. He recalled how she had begged, not for her life, or even for that of her children, but for mercy for the town and its citizens. As clearly remembered were the misadventures that had befallen all of them before they had at last found safe haven with Edward, Cecily's eldest surviving son who was now the king of England.

'My son the King will wish you two to be reconciled' Lady Cecily told Richard 'He will expect loyalty from you as from George.' Richard gave a snort of laughter 'Ha! George and loyalty, Mother! That will never be a matter to trust! Why, he sways with the wind!' 'Well now did you come to tell me how angry you are with George or did you come to speak of Lady Anne, lately Princess of Wales?' his mother asked her tone slightly acerbic.

Richard pulled up a little stool, and perched on it at his mother's side.

'I came, dear mother, to tell you that I found my Lady Anne in the place that you told me of, as you will have heard from Luke. And for her safety and also so that she should not feel under any obligation to me, I have placed her in a sanctuary where she is well provided for. Oh, mother!' 'You should have seen her! She was shut in a cellar and she is so thin and so dirty! It was so cold and she had only a ragged old shift to wear and now she has a cough! And I love her so much!' and he covered his face with his hands he sounded so grieved that his mother's heart bled for him

Cecily very gently took his hands from his face and held it in her own warm hands and she kissed him as if he were still a little child 'Now, my son, it is over. She is safe and I make no doubt that your brother Edward will arrange all so that you may wed her for I know that you two have loved each other since you were little children. Ned will see to it and make your marriage possible. You will do well by it.' She said 'Her inheritance …''Damn her inheritance!' The young man was instantly on his feet

'I will wed her with nothing but her shift! I love Anne not her inheritance!' he cried 'Now, my son, you must be sensible!' his mother told him 'You are a prince now, and besides there needs a Papal dispensation, for you and Lady Anne are close kindred.' his mother told him. 'Damn dispensations too! Papal or otherwise' declared her youngest son. 'I love Anne. I will wed Anne. She loves me. She will wed me. We promised it to each other when we were children!' And he rang the bell-pull by the hearth for a servant to come. 'Mother, I ask your pardon for my outburst. I am going to visit my lady now' Richard bowed and when the servant arrived he told him to alert Master Luke that his service was required.

Luke arrived and Richard kissed his mother's hand dutifully and then her cheek, smiling for he knew she would not be angry with him for long. 'Come, Luke' he said 'we will visit my lady and then we will wait upon my brother the king. Luke looked concerned 'What is it, man?' asked Richard 'Edward is a king not an ogre. He will not devour you!' 'Perhaps not,' complained Luke 'but I am ill dressed and ill equipped for a king's court.' His master looked him up and down. 'Why, man, you are clean and not tattered! You are as respectable as I am!' he said. 'Come now we must be off!' And he left the room with Luke following a little uncertainly behind him.

Cecily sighed. Richard was her youngest son and precious to her. She knew too what no-one, even those who were close to him did not: that he suffered from a problem with his spine. Oh, he would never mention it she knew that too. She did know that he had close discussions with his armourer and his tailor and that sometimes the wrinkle in his brow was deeper than at other times even when he had no worries. She knew that this was caused by pain. And yet it did not prevent Richard from doing everything that other youngsters did and now in spite of his problem he was a splendid warrior as brave as a lion and always used his head. 'Think first, then plan, then act' he always said and that was also what he did. She realized that although he was not so tall and gloriously handsome as her son Edward this young and precious lad was clever enough to be a great leader and good enough of soul to keep his friends and remain true to that which he believed. Nor was he addicted to women and good living for which as she sadly knew Edward had a notable propensity. Ah well, she thought, we will see what happens now!

Chapter 7.

A Marriage is Requested.

What did happen was that Richard went to speak with his brother Edward who was now king of England He was at his palace of Whitehall at the time so it was easy enough for Richard to go there. He and Luke hired a boat and were rowed up the Thames to Whitehall stairs, so avoiding the crowded streets and the mud.

Leaving Luke in the servants' hall Richard made his way to the Presence Chamber. Edward was not there but an official who recognized the king's younger brother took him to the privy apartments. Edward was working at some papers on a long table set under a window where the light was good. He looked up when Richard was announced. 'Well, brother, how do you?' he said and his eyes were bright and amused as they always were when he spoke with Richard, for his young brother was always so polite and so serious. 'Well, I thank your Grace' began Richard. 'Come now, what happened to 'Brother Ned'?' by now Edward was actually laughing. 'I feel that I must respect your position, your Grace' was the rejoinder. Edward grinned. 'Well now that you have, let's sit down and take some wine together' he went over to a bench seat in front of the great hearth. There was a fire in the hearth, although the weather wasn't cold, for this great palace was right beside the Thames and therefore damp in places. The kings private suite of rooms being, for access, closest to the Thames was one of the dampest. Edward poured some wine and they sat before the fire. 'Now what's the matter Diccon? You have your worried face today!' said the king. 'Oh Ned I have found my lady

Anne. Ned, I want your permission to marry her!' Richard's great need made the words come tumbling out, all thoughts of majesty and court manners left behind. 'Marry her?' Edward seemed surprised 'but she's a widow, Diccon' 'So was her Grace the Queen!' retorted Richard. Edward looked abashed 'Yes, well, she is the Queen' he said as if that explained everything. 'But she was plain Lady Grey when you married her!' said his brother 'Anne was married to the Lancaster Prince of Wales.' The king sounded testy. 'Lady Grey was a Lancastrian widow also. Ned, I love Anne' replied Richard. He was feeling very nervous and his right eye twitched a little. 'Yes, but why marry Anne Neville? I could find you another bride.' said Edward. The younger brother looked even more serious 'Ned I have told you. I love her. I have always loved her. She loves me and we decided to marry when I was at Middleham with her father.' 'You were children!' exclaimed Edward. 'Why, you are not twenty years old yet! And you must know that George is claiming all Anne's inheritance through his own marriage to her sister?'

Richard stood up. He was quite a lot shorter than his oldest living brother but then, Edward was very tall indeed: taller than anyone else in their family, so Richard found it easier to speak to Edward when he was standing up and Ned was sitting down. 'I know George wants her inheritance. I have just rescued her from the kitchen of a bawdy house where George had hidden her.' Richard's voice was challenging 'I don't care about the riches. I just care about Anne. Give me leave to marry her, your Grace and I will take her with only a shift to her name.' His eyes were so serious and so blue that Edward was quite taken aback. 'God be loved! You scare me sometimes, Diccon, you are so intense!' 'I do not mean to be arrogant. But if you had seen my poor lady when I found her, she was cold, dirty, ragged, a kitchen slut in a whorehouse....' Richard found he could not go on, his voice shook and he was afraid he might burst into tears.

Edward looked long and hard at his youngest brother. He rose to his feet, all two yards and more of him, and went back to his work table. 'I shall have to pacify George' he said 'and there is her mother too, pestering me for lands and so on. You know all their lands and holdings were confiscated to the Crown when the Earl was attainted. Now our brother George, who is always greedy, wants all of them. But if you are so set upon the poor lass I will settle George. Marry your Anne since you love her so much for I know how love bites and stings!' he laughed, 'My poor Richard! I am sorry for the trouble that you have had. Had I but known of George's deeds against the lady Anne I would have dealt with it myself but since you have found her and rescued her, no doubt it will have strengthened the bond between you. A kitchen maid you say, not one of the women of the house?' 'Not that, your Grace, just a kitchen maid. George at least saved her that much' Richard sounded bitter.

'Nay, now, go and marry your love. Hold the wedding ceremony but keep it quiet and away from too many prying eyes for we don't want to upset our brother of Clarence any more than we can help. As to the lands and so on I will see to that, too.' He turned to his papers. 'There is the mother' his voice was cold 'she harasses me. I don't know what to do with her!' Richard was silent for a few moments then he said 'Give her some of her late lord's holdings so that she has some small income and she can come to live with Anne and me. Anne loves her mother and they were ever close. I will look after both of them!'

Again, the king looked long and hard at his brother. 'You seem to have planned it all.' He said. His youngest brother, now

38

looking much less serious, told him 'Oh, I have, Ned. I know Anne will want her mother with her and I knew about the lands and holdings so it seemed common sense to make a household for the three of us. You want me up in the North Country and Anne and her mother loved to live at Middleham so we will make it our home. I will keep the North for you and make sure the Scots do not invade. While I was there, learning my craft as a knight, I made friends amongst the local people. I like them for they are plain speaking folk and trustworthy if they take to you, so it will be easy to govern so long as I am fair minded! And Ned – thank you!' He dropped to one knee and kissed his bothers hand. 'I will keep the North for you, my brother, my King. Loyalty will bind me to you, for I honour you as head of our House as well as my country's King. And I am full of gratitude that you allow me to wed Lady Anne.' Too full of emotion to say more he left the room, collected Luke and they made their way back down Whitehall Stairs to find a boat to take them back to his mother's house. Edward returned to his papers and his business as king; but finding it tiresome he went to look for another, much pleasanter, pass-time elsewhere in the palace.

Chapter 8

A Marriage is Made.

Lady Cecily was sitting sewing with her maids. They were making a new altar frontal for the reburial of her late husband the Duke York. King Edward had promised a proper funeral for his father. She had wondered much about her youngest son and his plans for marriage with the daughter of the late earl of Warwick. They were related of course for she had herself been a Neville and Anne and Richard were second cousins and Cecily had reminded Richard of this but he had refused to listen. He wasn't usually so intransigent especially with her. Indeed he was the most level headed of all her sons – all her sons! Thinking of them reminded her of her oldest boy, Edmund, butchered at the hands of Margaret the late King Henry's queen and her followers after the battle of Wakefield. Edmund had been so young and Cecily had never recovered from the shock of losing both her husband and her oldest son at the same time. But she was too proud to let her hurt be seen; she nursed it within her heart and held her head high. She remained proudly upright and seemingly calm even when she and her younger children had been made prisoners. She had stood at the market cross in Ludlow town square with her children gathered around her skirts and while she had requested mercy for the townspeople she had not deigned to beg for herself or her family. Mercy was not shown. Margaret of Anjou knew no mercy. Well, she was well paid for her lack of it now! Waiting for Richard to return from seeing Edward, Cecily was concerned. Edward had married in secret and his mother was not entirely approving of his choice. Nor was she certain that the marriage was actually legal. 'Nobody present at the wedding but Edward, Elizabeth, her mother and a priest whose name I don't know!' she thought. Without a dispensation would Anne's marriage to Richard be legal?

'My sons!' she exclaimed to herself 'Ned, and now Diccon both, marrying hastily, and George, demanding things that are not his by rights! How shall I ever keep them all safe, and soundly wed?' someone came tapping on her chamber door. It was her maid who came in, breathless. 'Madam, Lord Richard has arrived!' Cecily looked from her casement, from whence she could see into the courtyard. He sprang from his horse and dashed into the house, arriving panting from the stairs, at his mother's door. 'Come in, my son!' she said. He looked flushed and happy 'Ned has given permission!' he cried joyfully 'he says I may marry Anne!' 'And have you asked permission of her lady mother?' his mother inquired.' He crowed 'I don't have to! The king has given permission and Anne has already accepted me! Mother, I am so very happy! But Ned says we must wed with no great splendour or show for fear of angering George'. He sat down beside her chair, and took her hand 'Mother! You will be at my wedding?' he sounded like a little boy again she thought, asking for sweetmeats! But he had never been a greedy child, and she knew in her secret heart that, while she mourned Edmond, was proud of Ned, and fond of George, for all his ways, yet this, her youngest son, was the best of them all, the most attached to her, and perhaps her best beloved. He had never told little lies when he was young so that he would not be reprimanded for getting dirty or for breaking something. She knew he was steadfast and truthful and that he doted on her and on his brothers, especially on Ned, and on his sisters, too. She herself also loved Anne, for she was a gentle, quiet girl, equally as simply truthful as Diccon. 'Well

41

my son, you have my blessing!' she told him. 'Am I to see your bride?' Richard kissed his mother's hand and her brow, 'Of course, Mother, I will bring her here to you. She will need help' Cecily nodded. She knew that Ann's mother was in Sanctuary and refused to come out. Brides needed a mother-figure to help with wedding plans.

Later that day Richard visited Anne and explained that the King had given his permission for them to be married. His eyes were a bright deep blue as he said. 'We may not have a great show, my love,' he said 'for the king my brother does not wish to anger my brother of Clarence but my mother will be there and I have friends too who will wish to see us wed' She smiled 'Yes! All those fine young men whose friendship you won while at Middleham! Oh, Richard, my Richard! My love! I am so happy. You cannot know how terrible my life was until you came to my rescue for I thought I should die in that place. The people here have been very kind to me but I shall be happy indeed to see my Aunt your lady mother, and Oh! I cannot wait to be your wife! How soon may we wed? We have loved each other for so long!' He took her hand, 'It will not be long, my Anne!' he looked at her and his deep set blue eyes were twinkling with joy. 'We must have the banns called and I think you need a new gown! And I know my lady mother will wish to have a great many discussions with you. Shall we go to her now? It is nearing dark so we will be less likely to be seen and I have discreet guards posted. Besides I have Luke here, waiting for us and we can be sure he will see that no harm befalls us!'

So they went by the river to Lady Cecily who greeted them both with great warmth and joy. She found some beautiful fabric for Anne's wedding dress and promised that her own sewing woman would make it up 'Why, a kerchief would make a smock for you so thin you are become!' she said, worried by Anne's slenderness and pallor 'Never fear, Mother' said Richard, 'it is only from being in that dreadful cellar. Soon Anne will be plump and rosy again' 'Oh, yes, my lady, I will be very well, very soon!' said Anne, making a pretty curtsey to Lady Cecily. 'No my dear don't be formal with me! Come and kiss me, for I am to be your good-mother!' and Cecily took the thin, pale girl in her arms and kissed her on both cheeks. 'We could have the wedding here in my house, if you wish' she said 'George does not visit me often as does Diccon when he is able, so we will be safe. Who will be your groom's man, Diccon?' her son thought for a moment and then he said 'Why, Luke of course, for he helped me find and rescue my bride!' 'A good choice; Luke is a fine man' his mother said 'and who will marry you?' 'Your house priest is a good man and he will be silent.' said Richard.

So it was arranged and as soon as the banns were called and the bridal gown sewn, the wedding took place.

However, the King insisted that his youngest brother be married in Westminster Abbey Church for he wished the world to know that he was most certainly King and a puissant monarch, whose family were important to both him and the country

On the twelfth day of July in the year of Our Lord 1472, Luke stood groom's man and the youngest of Cecily's ladies attended the bride. The chapel in which the marriage was to be held was decked with green boughs for good fortune and the priest wore a fine cope worked and presented by the groom's mother.

Anne came into the chapel on the arm of Cecily's steward, a careful man who had served her for many years and was completely trustworthy.

The bride looked beautiful.

Her face was much pinker now and she had gained a little of the weight that she had lost. Her hair hung like wings of gold about her shoulders and the dressmaker had made sure that the gown fitted her exactly; the beautiful pale blue silk rustled and the under dress was of mulberry coloured satin for those were Richard's colours.

Instead of his usual rather sombre work-a-day garments, Richard was also richly dressed in mulberry slashed with pale blue, to match his bride.

Luke stood with Richard to await the arrival of the bride and heard the intake of breath as Richard caught the first sight of her. He felt the younger man tremble but when he looked at him Luke saw that it was with joy. Anne was also joyful and when Richard had placed the wedding ring, deeply engraved with his crest, on her finger little tears of sheer happiness shone in her eyes. Pronounced man and wife together they embraced most tenderly. Lady Cecily was delighted, and she too had tears of joy on her cheeks and embraced both of them, crying 'My dear, dear children!' Smiling broadly Luke shook his master's white but strong and calloused hand and bowed over the bride's tiny soft one. They left the chapel a happy knot of well contented people.

Chapter 9.

Their Wedding Night

Richard's mother had had a sumptuous meal prepared for them
all with Luke and the priest sitting with them at her son's
express wish. Cecily's ladies played and sang and they all
danced including the priest, who was young as yet for his
calling and still retained the manners of a courtly gentleman.
As soon as it was polite to do so the newly weds slipped away.
Lady Cecily had a chamber prepared for them with a beautiful
bed hung with rich curtains furnished with feather mattress and
pillows with an elegantly embroidered bedspread over the soft
fleecy blankets. Covered with fine lawn cloth, food and wine
stood ready laid out on a side table, in case they became
hungry or thirsty. In the great hearth a fire was laid, ready to be
lit should the night turn chill.
Anne's waiting woman had followed softly behind her mistress
and now she stepped forward to remove the cape that hung
from Anne's shoulders. Richard signed to her to stop. 'I will
assist Lady Anne. You may leave us.' he said, gently. He
removed the long cape and then he helped Anne out of the
ornate wedding gown laying it carefully on a bench seat. She
was shy but he reminded her that he had recently seen her in a
much worse garment than the fine shift she now wore. Then
effortlessly in spite of his slender build, he lifted her in his
arms and laid her on the great bed, drawing the curtains around
her. She waited as he disrobed. Her heart was knocking against
her ribs, for she loved him and although her marriage to the
young prince Edward had not been consummated, she knew
what to expect. Richard opened the curtain and slid naked into

the bed beside her. 'You are shivering my Love!' he said. His voice was a little different to its usual level tone and was slightly husky. He put his arms around her and holding her tightly but gently he kissed her. First her eyes, then her lips then he kissed her throat and felt her heart beat there. His own blood quickened. He held her a little closer still and she felt his desire for her. She returned his kisses but then she drew away a little 'Why, what is it, my love?' he asked his eyes puzzled 'do you not love me?' 'I do love you my Richard' she said 'but although I am a widow I am a virgin'. 'And do you think that I will hurt you?' he asked his lips on her neck. 'I don't know.' her voice was small and shaky. He laughed very softly, and very gently he began to caress her. 'It is not so bad, my Anne, do not fear for I will be most gentle! I am not a widow but I do know what to do and I can promise that you will enjoy love in our marriage!' As they clung together she felt him harden against her and suddenly as he kissed her again and caressed one small breast, she felt as if she would melt, and she gasped. Very gently and with utmost consideration, delicacy and care, he took his wife. She felt that heaven had come to earth. Richard was with her, inside her. He was her wedded husband. He whom she had loved for so long and who had rescued her from that dreadful cellar! Richard too was full of emotion. At last his true love was his bride, his wife!

'I have awaited this for so long' he told her stroking her hair 'I can hardly believe it, my Anne! My Lady of Love! She nestled close to him, her head on his breast, her tears of joy spilling onto to her cheek. Kissing her he tasted the salt 'Why, what is this? Weeping, my dearest' 'Only with joy!' she told him. He laid her gently back against the pillows 'Rest now, my beloved.' he told her 'Tomorrow we will begin to prepare to go home!' Anne's eyes widened 'Home?' she asked 'Ned has made me governor of the North, so we will live at Middleham. Will you be happy there?' he said. Anne could hardly believe it exclaiming 'My own home!' then she thought for a moment 'What of my lady mother? She is still in sanctuary and Isabel does not see her............' her voice trailed away. 'Ah, but I have permission for her to live with us. You will need her when our son arrives.' Richard sounded very sure. Anne was now too happy and said she would not sleep at all because she was so excited. Her husband left the bed and brought her wine and little dried fruits. He also brought warm water and a towel and gently washed her so that she might be comfortable after their love making. She blushed 'Even my ladies do not do that.' she told him 'But I am not one of your ladies. I am your husband' he said, triumphantly 'I can do anything for you, and I will' he kissed her again, wound his arms round her and she, amazed at his strength and muscularity, cuddled up against him and slept.

Richard looked down at her golden head; he could barely believe it was Anne he held after all the years he had loved her and longed for this moment! He thought of that other chestnut haired woman, introduced to him by Ned, when he was sixteen or so. He had not really loved her but she was kind and accommodating and he had enjoyed their connexion. They had stayed together long enough to have John and Katherine his two children. He loved these base-born children and would do all he could for them but although he had liked her he had not wished to wed their mother – and she had always known that this was so and that he had provided and always would provide for her and for them. It had just been that his splendid brother Ned had so much wanted him to 'become a man!' He sighed, for he would have to tell Anne about the children especially as they were living at Sheriff Hutton not so very far from Middleham where he intended to live with Anne.

He wondered if she would allow them to live with her as part of his family but did not think he dared ask too much of her! Well, he was only three months short of twenty he thought and more than ready for life as a great lord and the husband of a great lady. He kissed the soft golden hair of his sweet wife's sleeping head and then he, too, slept.

Outside their chamber door, his truckle bed across the threshold, Luke told his beads before he also slept.

Chapter 10.

Crosby's Place and Happiness

Anne was so happy! Reunited with Richard whom she had
loved since she was a child and with her beautiful Aunt Cecily
she was at last at peace safely married and once more living in
comfort. The cough that she had developed during her sojourn
in the cellar was an irritation but no more than that. Her mother
was still in sanctuary but Richard had promised that she should
come to live with them as soon as he could arrange with the
king that they could go to the North. She could not bring
herself to like George, her brother in law of Clarence, but she
had been reconciled with Isabel her sister who had not been
party to what George had done to her.
Court life was too stiff and formal and Anne could feel too
many cross-currents just below the polite surface and she found
it very uncomfortable, as did Richard. However, since he was
now in a position of great trust with the King his brother
Richard had to stay in London for a while longer. Anne often
managed to keep away from Court and all its controversies
either with Lady Cecily at Baynard's Castle or at Crosby's
Place, Richard's house in London, recently leased so that he
had a home for his wife and himself. This was a place where
they could be private and alone. The more they saw of each
other the more their love grew.
In Crosby's Place Anne was happiest of all making a home for
the young man whom she loved so much and who in return
loved her so tenderly.
She knew now, as she had guessed for a long time, that he
suffered pain from his spine which she now also knew had

become twisted. He was of a much more slender build than either Edward or George who were big boned men, and his determination to excel in martial arts had cost him dear for he had begun to train with a man's weapons at too young an age. Cecily had told Anne of how Richard, her youngest son, had promised at a ridiculously young age, that he would become a mighty warrior so that he could suppress all traitors and defend his mother and his sisters!

He had also worked very hard at the art of war, learning tactics and reading of the great conquerors like Julius Caesar, Alexander the Great, Edward the First, Edward the Third, and any other of the heroes of whom he could find records, and of those whom they had overcome too, so that he knew what to avoid and not to do, as well as what he should study to accomplish. Anne never mentioned his spine but when they lay together warm and comfortable in the great bed, she would gently massage her husband's back using sweet oils and ointments. He did not refer to this either but always kissed her and stroked her golden hair when she had finished. She knew how to soothe his aches and he was grateful both for her help and for her understanding silence.

Dressed, no one would know of his problem for he was of average height, a mite taller than his brother George, and wearing the right armour he could fight with any man. He knew that with good skill and high courage he could prevail. Yet Richard loved peace. He loved to walk in the garden of his house his beautiful Lady Anne on his arm, talking of their plans to leave London as soon as King Edward allowed them to go to the North. 'I do not like Court life' Anne said, as they walked on the grass one day 'There are too many undercurrents. I never know what your brother will do next and I am a little frightened' 'Afraid of Ned?' Richard was a little shocked for he adored his oldest brother. 'No, not really of the King, although he is so tall and so splendidly dressed and has so loud a voice!' she replied 'It is George. I have seen how he looks at me - and at you!' 'George will always do the unexpected,' her husband said 'he always has done.' They walked on a little way, then he stopped 'He will not do anything to hurt you, sweetheart' he told his wife 'for he knows that I am on my guard; and there is nothing more for him to desire, he has all your father's lands and holdings bar a very little. I bargained to have you as my wife and I have you. Let him enjoy what he has while he may. I know my brother – he is likely to make a foolish move even now!' He walked on, shaking his head sadly.

He had been the youngest of Lady Cecily's many children but now there were only his sisters and two of his brothers, Edward and George, left. The others had died in infancy, except Edmund the oldest, who Richard barely remembered, who had died fighting alongside their father at Sandal Castle when Richard was himself a little boy. He wanted to be part of a family and did not like the tension with his brother of Clarence. His sisters were all married and Margaret was far away in Burgundy. As they went back inside Richard turned Anne to face him 'I do not care for Court life either, my love. I will speak again to my brother the king.'

Thinking this a good moment Richard began to explain to his wife that he already had a son and a daughter. Shyly he told her that he had a confession to make to her before they went northwards to live. She laid a finger over his mouth. 'My dearest Love' she said 'if you are going to tell me about Katherine and John please know that I am already aware of them. I know that they live at Sheriff Hutton and I think it will be a good nursery for our other children when they arrive. And none of our children will be without siblings so do not be ashamed for they are after all of royal blood, having you for their father!' Richard was taken aback 'You know about them?' 'Yes, of course I know. Everyone in our family knows. We do not consider them a disgrace. They are your offspring so they are a part of our family. I will love them as I will love our other children when they arrive!' her husband looked at her in awe 'You amaze me every time I look at you!' he cried 'And now you accept my base born children! Anne, my Anne, you are the most generous lady I have ever known of!' and he kissed her tenderly. She clung to him 'I love you, my Richard!' she told him, 'and I will love your children because they are yours.' He picked her up and carried her silently to their bed chamber where in still in silence he worshipped her in the act of love.

Chapter 11.

Lady Cecily's Concerns

Lady Cecily did not approve of the King's wife. She had not known of the marriage and only knew of it as a hole and corner affair which had taken place in secret. The lady was a widow and, what was more, the widow of one of the Lancastrian knights who had fought against Edward as well as against his father. So lady Cecily distrusted her. Then there were her seemingly endless relations – all of whom it seemed, were in desperate need of places at Court. Edward did not seem able to deny the pale, light-brown haired woman anything. Cecily wondered about the Lady Eleanor Talbot with whom Edward had seemed so smitten and whom he had professed to love. That fair lady had withdrawn to a convent but Edward had still bestowed much good land upon her. Cecily wondered why. He had taken another mistress very soon and Eleanor Talbot had vanished into her nunnery. Then suddenly, just as a marriage with a French Princess was being arranged for him Edward had declared himself a married man and introduced Lady Grey as his wife! Cecily felt that there was a mystery about the Woodville woman that would one day be found to be shameful. Well, Edward was King now and the whey faced slut was his queen. She was a greedy, scheming woman who had Edward by his nose! Cecily knew her sons well and Edward had few secrets from his mother though he might not realize it.
She worried about George too: just being Duke of Clarence did not suit him, he wanted to be much nearer to the throne than that – he had joined with Warwick in rebellion because he thought there was a chance that he could be king. He had even

started a rumour about Edward being a bastard and not her husband's child at all. True, one day when she had been very cross with him she had called Edward that - but it was in anger and she did not mean it. But of course George had jumped on it! He would. He also boasted to his mother that he knew of something which would confound and ruin his older brother and Cecily thought that she might know what he had in mind. But she did not ask him to elucidate nor did she discuss it with anyone.

She sighed. Poor unhappy George! He was never satisfied although he had a beautiful bride and all her inheritance. And he was green with envy of his brother Richard. That was because Ned trusted Diccon while he did not trust George; which was hardly surprising given the insurrection. She had worried about George when he had been imprisoned in the Tower of London and had begged Edward to release him. Eventually matters were patched up between her sons but Cecily feared that the patch was growing thin.

Cecily thanked God for her youngest son. Richard had married well. Anne was a real noblewoman as well as his one great love and they were happy. He was trustworthy and loyal to his brother the King and he worked hard to reconcile George and Edward too. He cared about his mother and visited her often seeking her advice as well as her company. Cecily worried that Lady Anne seemed too slender and had a cough, but there was no doubt that she and Richard had a good marriage. It was sad that they would be going to Middleham to live but it would be possible for her to visit them and she knew she would be welcomed. Now given high commands, Richard worked hard for the King and always gave of his best. She was glad that he had Luke with him because most of his friends were in or around York so that she felt the warm companionship with this slightly older and quiet man was good for Richard. She had had speech with Luke and liked him – he was forthright and pleasant and, she guessed, pious, for she had noticed a book in his pocket and when she mentioned it and he had pulled it out to show her she had seen that it was a Psalter. Cecily sighed contentedly and settled back to embroidering her late husbands' blazon on the altar frontal that she and her ladies were making.

Chapter 12.

1473 And Middleham

At last, Richard and Anne had been able to go to Middleham. They were joyful to be back in the dales of Yorkshire where they had first met and where their love had first taken root and then bloomed. Now it was in full bloom and about to bring forth fruit for Anne had come to speak to Richard as he pored over State papers one day. 'My lord!' she said 'Why, my love! Why do you call me lord? What is it dearest?' he looked very worried. 'I have some news for you, my Richard'. Anne spoke quietly. 'What news, dearest wife?' he asked. Anne smiled. 'We shall have a sibling for Katherine and John' she said. Richard felt stunned 'A child? We are to have a child?' he asked. Anne nodded, joy in her eyes. 'Yes, my Richard. I am with child! Is it not wonderful?' Her husband took her gently into his arms and kissed her. 'My sweet Anne, how I love you – I will see to it that you are well cared for' he said 'I shall ask my mother to tell me who should come to assist you. And your lady mother will, I am certain, know what you should and do what you should eat and...' laughing, Anne stopped him, her forefinger on his mouth, 'Hush, dearest! All will be well!' she said 'Then let us go to the chapel and give thanks to God' said her husband.

So they went to kneel together at the little altar in the chapel, with lighted candles in their hands and prayers of gratitude on their lips and in their hearts. It was chilly in the tiny stone place and Anne coughed a little. Richard raised her to her feet and wrapped his cloak around her 'You must not take cold, my Anne' he said and he led her away to their warm chamber.

They talked for a little while making plans for their future and that of their child.

Richard had work to do and he left Anne to sew quietly by the fire. It was colder in the North but the air was cleaner than in the streets of London and Richard thought his wife seemed healthier for which he thanked God. He sought out Luke and asked him if he had read any books of medical matters 'A few, my Lord, they are not so frequently found as religious works' 'Why do you call me lord, Luke?' asked Richard ' I thought that we had decided on 'master'?'. 'Ah, but you were not so great then as now you are! I must be more...' 'No! I wish all between us to be as it was' said Richard 'for we are friends, Luke!' 'Very well, Master Richard' Luke's eyes twinkled as he looked at his friend. 'I will find what you need for your lady's lying-in!' 'Now, how do you know of that?' Richard was surprised. 'I have seen the change in the Lady Anne's face' said Luke 'such a secret and joyful look can mean only one thing!' Richard was pleased 'Yes, thanks be to God, we shall have a child.' He said. Luke then spoke very carefully 'My lord, my master and friend, I have to ask a boon of you'. 'Why, Luke, ask for whatever you wish for I will give it if it lies in my power to do so.' Replied Richard wondering what it could be that Luke needed.

Taking a deep breath Luke said 'My dear master, when I joined you, I said that I would remain with you until you had found Lady Anne. Now, with your leave, I wish to return to my home town, there to become a monk. I have left it late but my calling has not left me. May I go?' Richard looked serious and the slight frown that came to his brow when he was thoughtful or worried made its appearance. 'My friend, if you truly have a vocation, I must not hinder you' he said, sadly 'although I shall miss you greatly for we have been close friends.' Luke looked down thought for a moment and then he said 'Master Richard, I will pray for you and your lady and your whole family. And should you be in need I will come to you. Perhaps if you were to write a letter which I can show to the Father Abbott he may give me permission to come to you when you need me. I shall not fear the journey.' Richard looked more cheerful. 'I trust that you will let me know that you have arrived in safety and I will provide a bodyguard' Luke laughed 'No, my dear master, I shall need no bodyguard. You forget that I trained as a knight!' he said 'And of course I will write to you. And I hope that you will send me tidings when you Lady's child is born. May I go soon? I wish to travel in good weather.' 'May you go with God's blessing as well as mine' said his master 'Brother Luke! I shall not forget you, and do you remember me!' the two men shook hands and then embraced each other warmly. Luke set off the next day, in bright sunshine on foot, for he had left the handsome grey gelding as a gift to his master. He took with him a letter from the Duke of Gloucester instructing any one in authority over Luke to allow him leave to visit the Duke of Gloucester whenever that Duke should wish it.

Chapter 13.

1476: Edward of Middleham.

Anne had given birth to a son. They had named him Edward for his uncle the King and no prouder parents ever graced Yorkshire. Or the world, come to that! Anne was frail but was well enough to be churched at the usual time. Richard was overjoyed to have a legitimate son and was often to be seen dandling the little one on his knee while he read State Papers for he delighted in this child and in his lady Anne. However Anne was never as well as she would have been had she not endured that time in the damp cellar. Her husband worried constantly and was always seeking ways to make her well. He had fresh fish kept in a specially dug and constructed fish-keep in the floor of the great kitchen and fruit and vegetables were brought from the orchards and farms nearby. He quite often hunted for he could keep a careful military watch on the countryside at the same time, and if he was lucky with his hunting he brought home venison, hares and game birds for their table and he hoped that in time good food and the clean Yorkshire air would help his wife to become stronger.

Keeping the country under surveillance was a necessity because the Scots would raid over the border if they could and local families made feuds among themselves; it all had to be watched over. Richard gradually made the local lords as well as the gentry and commoners know that he was firmly in charge. He was fair-minded, gave good and impartial judgements when needed and lived his personal life quietly. There was no one with a grudge whom he did not personally interview to find out why they bore it; no family was allowed to harass another. The young duke protected women and children helping them in many ways in times of need or danger and he would not tolerate men who bullied their wives and daughters. All this certainly kept him busy and he was often too far from Middleham to return to his home and his wife, when night fell. But he always prepared Anne in advance if he intended to go so far away, and always made sure that all was safe and that Anne was well served. Having her mother with them was a great help for Anne had someone to talk with and to ask about her child and how best he should be cared for.

It was not long before Richard had won all the hearts that counted for anything in the North. He had also to ensure that the Scots stayed in Scotland but he even managed that, and made a pact with the Scottish king. Men were proud to be amongst his men at arms and to serve him, and even the gentry liked and admired their dashing but serious minded young Duke. He had made a good impression on the crusty old lords of the North too, and although they did not love him as much as others did yet they knew him to be a fair dealing and hard working man who asked no more of any man than he would do himself, so he won from them a grudging respect and cooperation.

Anne also made a good impression for she was very young and beautiful, rather shy and very gentle. She was also generous with her charitable works which she handled sensibly, not making a big show but finding out what was needed and where it was most needed. Her personal life was, like her husband's quiet and obviously homely. She could be seen walking in Middleham village with her child and his nurse and a lady and this was sometimes her mother. She bought all that she needed from the area in which she lived not sending South for luxuries but purchasing good woollen cloth that was made locally and linen the same. Her sweet nature her beauty and loyalty to Yorkshire and its crafts-people won all hearts. So they were both well thought of and well loved.

And they had each other and their little son. Richard's other two children lived close to them and as well as that a couple of lads were in Richard's household just as Richard himself had been in Anne's father's household, to learn how to be knights and gentlemen. Thus it was a large and happy family that lived in and around the great castle at Middleham. Richard was content. He would have liked his own mother with them too, but she was unwilling to leave her own houses and her own charitable works. Lady Cecily had somewhat fallen out with her son Edward, king though he was, because as she disapproved of the marriage he had made and so preferred not to be at Court. Richard missed her, for he loved his mother. Another joy for Richard was that he was reunited with some of those lads with whom he learnt when he was young at Middleham and many of these friendships were to be life-long.

Life was busy and for a long while Richard did not go London more than a couple of times. He was so busy keeping the North for King Edward. He was delighted to have such employment and to have a family around him and his delight flowed out to those with whom he came into contact. His nickname 'Diccon' became a bye-word for anything good, just as years later the words 'King Dick' meant that something was more than just good!

The Duke of Gloucester young as he was, was known to be a reliable ally, a good friend and an impartial judge and such a one as had rarely been known in those parts. His totally happy home life had much to do with this.

Chapter 14.

Trumpets and Alarams. 1475

A messenger from King Edward arrived at Middleham. Richard and Anne were dining with their family but as soon as he knew of the messenger's arrival Richard wiped his hands and making his excuses left the table at once to see this man.

'I bring a letter my lord' the messenger had obviously ridden fast and furiously to get to him and when Richard saw the King's seal he told the fellow to go to the kitchens to get food and drink, while he read the letter. He was not happy at the contents. Edward's advisers had prevailed upon him to raise taxes to fund war on France. Richard did not agree with this plan. Although an accomplished warrior and a good leader he was a peace loving man and he preferred to settle differences with discussion and diplomacy. But, he sighed to himself, he was not the King!

Richard was commanded to accompany the King and George Duke of Clarence to make war on France. What, Richard wondered, was Edward doing taking Clarence with him? And who could have persuaded Edward to go to war for here was a man who had undoubtedly been a great commander but who was now, Richard knew, getting fat from laziness. There seemed few good reasons for Edward to make this decision!

Going back to the table Richard asked Anne to go to their private chamber with him. Seeing him looking so concerned Anne asked him 'What has happened, my Richard? Why are you so troubled?' 'My dearest Love, I am called to confer with the king' he told her, 'and then to France to fight alongside my brothers.' 'But why?' cried the lady, 'what has happened to make the king take this decision?' 'That I do not know, Sweetheart, but I must ride to London. I will try to advise Ned but I fear that the Woodville family are somehow behind this folly of his and they will be hard for me to work against'

Anne was paler than usual 'I am frightened my Richard. What will happen if you do not come home again?' 'Never fear, my Lady of Love, I will come back to you whatever happens. I am a soldier: it is my trade and was taught me by your father. He taught me well and I take due note of all his teaching. Never fear. But I am concerned that Edward may be under a bad influence.' 'If it is that of his queen it will not be a good influence, Richard. I do not trust Elizabeth and neither does my lady Cecily our mother. But so that you come safe home I do not care what the king does.' Richard gave a short harsh laugh 'I will find out when I get to him, Sweeting, but I fear I must go now. I have to reply to his letter and then I must ride out to raise troops for him. That will be a hard task for what have Yorkshire lads to do with London or France!' He kissed her briefly 'Go and finish your dinner, my sweet lady, and tell no-one of what we have said.' He left her and went to his study and Anne returned to the dinner table.

Richard re-read the King's letter and then in his neat and careful script he replied to it so that the messenger could take it to the King, starting at dawn the next day. In order not to lose time Richard then wrote a declaration for his Herald to make in all the towns under his jurisdiction. At the top was Richard's own Blanc Sanglier and his motto 'Loyauté Me Lie'. The white boar and the motto, 'Loyalty Binds Me', had become a frequent sight in the Dales as it was in North Wales and all the other lands for which Richard was responsible.

He also wrote to the individual lords and gentlemen whom he personally knew and upon whom he could rely to answer the call of duty. To those who were beyond fighting age he wrote asking for men or supplies only and not for their own active service. He loved and honoured his brother the King but he was unhappy about the enterprise. However he soon raised a troop and they were armed and ready to fight for their Duke of Gloucester if for nothing else, as they marched off to the meeting place appointed.

Anne and Richard had taken a sweet, sad farewell of each other and had clung together closely in the days and nights before he left to join Edward and George to embark for France. The love between them was a meaningful entity in their lives. It had become a spiritual as well as a carnal bond. 'I think I can almost hear your thoughts, my Anne' Richard said to her one day as they sat quietly, she with her sewing and he with his lists of arms needed 'I am sure that you can, my Richard!' she said, and she looked up from her needle and smiled at him. 'Come my wife' he said, holding out his hand to her 'come to our bed and let us be one in love, for it may be long before we can again lie together' and she got up and took his outstretched hand and they went into their bed chamber with the door firmly closed.

Later as he held her quietly in his arms, both of them sated with love, he said 'It is like a thanksgiving prayer, my Lady of Love, when I am with you' 'And I thank God for you, my Richard' said Anne, nestling closer to her husband's bare chest 'I did not believe such happiness and such one-ness could exist. You have shown me such care and courtesy. And every time that I read your 'Loyauté me lie' I remember how your loyal love rescued me from hell!' She kissed what part of him she could reach which happened to be a rib and he laughed a little because it tickled, so then they both laughed and rolled over together in the great bed, and found themselves again locked in an embrace that was both gentle and passionate 'Oh dear God! How I love you! AAAnne!' he cried in extreme of bliss.

Chapter 15.

The Shameful Peace.

Richard rode straight home to Middleham after the dealings at Picquingy.

Ned had not fought. They had sailed to France with a large army all ready for battle. But Edward had thought better of it. He had made peace with the French King Louis, and had sold his honour by agreeing not to fight in return for a large sum of money.

It was true that the French had the worst of the bargain but Richard was ashamed and angry. He had not really wanted a war, but to go France with money from the huge taxes and 'benefices' that Ned had levied on his people, and then not to strike a single blow but to let the French buy him off seemed shameful to Richard. He was sickened to see the great lords of England taking bribes from King Louis and he had refused such things. He had accepted an invitation to dinner with the French king, for not to do so would have been an insult on behalf of King Edward but he did not wish to fraternise and he was upset when he found fine horses and pieces of massy silverware, intended as gifts from king Louis, awaiting him when he took his leave. Richard of Gloucester made it perfectly clear that he could not be bought or pensioned by France and he made straight for home with his contingent of men.

He took with him a lasting picture of Edward, florid faced and already over-weight, dressed like a peacock in gorgeous silks and velvet with the Fleur de Lys the symbol of the kingship of France sported in his cap, riding to meet the French King.

Louis was dressed as if he had rummaged in the laundry bag. The recollection made Richard feel rather sick. His splendid, great-hearted, beloved, oldest brother had turned into a fat and scheming politician who thought only of hard cash and show.

Richard knew that politics were important and he was not unmindful that Edward's ploys with King Louis had meant that there were no casualties and had given Ned some financial security for his rule, but the people of England, who still basked in the remembered glory of Agincourt, had paid good money all ranks of them, for a fight with the French and Edward had sold out. Nor was he likely to return his people's money! Richard could feel in his bones that there would be repercussions.

George of Clarence along with many other English lords had done well from the outing but he was still dissatisfied and moody. He could turn on the charm when he needed to but his family were beginning to know how false that charm could be. And George had fallen out with the queen and her brothers. That was fatal.

Richard was glad to get away from all that false show and pomp and he marched his contingent of Yorkshire stalwarts safely home at the double. He had given instructions that there be no fanfare at Middleham when he arrived for he wanted to surprise his wife!

Very quietly the duke of Gloucester rode into the postern gate of his home and giving his grey into the hands of a stable lad he softly mounted the stair, walked through the gallery and stood in the open door of the solar. It was September and the golden light of early autumn lit him from behind. She was sitting and sewing her hair pure gold in the sunlight and little Edward was playing on a rug on the floor with his toys spread around him. Richard watched for a moment then softly 'Anne!'

67

he said. At Richard's voice Anne started and turned round to look. 'Richard! My love, you are home!' she rejoiced and rose to meet him. He stepped forward his blue eyes shining and swept her into his arms. 'My lovely Anne!' he exclaimed 'How glad I am to be home!' 'Oh! I cannot tell you how happy I am! We all will be!' She cried. 'Don't tell anyone yet, my love' he begged, 'allow me to get out of this harness and spend a little time with you and Edward before we see anyone else.' 'I will help you to disarm.' Anne said. Her hands flew round the buckles and he was soon released from his armour. Then he strode over and picked up his three year old son 'Well now, my little man! And how do you, my son?' he asked fondly and the little boy chuckled and held his father's finger in a fat fist. A big dimpled smile developed and a small white flash told the doting father that his young son had another tooth coming through. 'Fader' said the little one. 'I tell him about his father all the time' said Lady Anne 'for I do not want him to forget you!' 'No fear of that! I will be here with you now, my sweet Love, and I will ensure that this young man behaves!' Richard reassured her. He pretended to be cross with Edward, wagging his forefinger at him but the little boy just laughed and held on to his father's leg 'Ride!' he demanded.

Richard picked him up and piggy-backed him around the chamber. Anne watched with her heart aching for she knew her husband's back would be sore from riding. He gave no sign of hurt, but he soon put the boy down and found a seat. 'Play with your soldiers my son' he said.. Then he held out an arm to Anne 'Come here, dearest love, and let me look at you!' she came to him, and was held gently in his strong and tender embrace. 'I am tired from my journey, my Lady of Love love, but if I rest now will you share my bed tonight?' he asked. 'We always sleep together, my husband?' she said, querying him

'Yes, dearest Anne, but I have been so far away for so long that I do not know if you still love me!' the deep set blue eyes were merry. 'Foolish man!' his wife pretended to admonish him 'Why would I not love you!' 'Then tonight you can show me how much you love me!' he said 'I have been so lonely, dear wife, and all for nothing but shame.' And he told her of the outcome of his travels.

Anne was puzzled. 'Why did the king go all that way with that great array only to take a bribe and then come home again?' she wondered. 'I am sure he had started with some intention of fighting' her husband said as he was busy taking off his doublet 'we made enough plans for attack, defence, retreat in fact everything necessary and lines of supply were set up. But then Ned just changed his mind. And of course the king of France was good at bribing the right men.' He shook his head as he put on a comfortable loose gown 'Anne, my brother has been led astray' he spoke sadly 'I fear that his wife and her family have made him a lover of soft living'. His wife agreed 'Yes. Even here we are told stories of his life. He eats too heartily and drinks deeply and he takes many young women to his bed. I will not call them 'mistresses' for they are only his for a night! It would seem that he cannot be faithful to Elizabeth in spite of being under her thumb. It must be simply lust for he does not keep these women. They are brought to him by his friend Lord Hastings or so we hear.'

Richard sighed. 'I fear it is a case of "How are the mighty fallen"' he said 'but let us forget that now, my Anne, and we will collect our family around us and rejoice that we are together once more. And not one of my good Yorkshire lads got so much as a scratch!' He kissed her and stood up stretching his limbs. It was good to be home. Bread was being baked and the smell rose up to meet him making him feel hungry. Anne called a servant to bring wine and white bread and cold meats for her husband and she watched with joy as he refreshed himself. Little Edward sat at his father's feet and every now and then Richard popped a morsel into the rosy mouth. 'He looks like you, my Anne!' he said, 'and he seems to have more appetite than you. My lady, you have lost weight your face is thinner! What ails you, my dear Love?' 'Only my lack of my husband' she told him, 'and now I am cured!' Sadly Richard noticed that she still had the little cough which had begun to worry her after her time in the cellar. He made a mental note to speak to their physician.

Chapter 16.

Reburial the late Richard Duke of York.

It was the year of Our Lord 1776 and King Edward who was flush with French money, decided that it was time that his late father and his older brother Edmund should be buried decently. Both had been hastily and unceremoniously laid in earth at Pontefract where they had both been killed after the battle of Wakefield, and that was more than a decade and a half ago.

Edward sent for Richard. When the letter commanding his presence at Court arrived for him Richard was still busy fending off the Scots. He answered Edward's letter at once and sent the messenger on his way. Then he went wearily to seek his wife. Anne was busy gathering herbs for making simples from the plants which grew in her little garden within the castle walls. Hearing his usual soft footfall approaching she looked up smiling. Then she saw the little lines between his eye brows and knew he was worried.

'What troubles you Richard, my love?' she asked. 'I have to go to speak with the king and I cannot truthfully spare the time. Nor do I relish going to that Court again!' he spoke ruefully and she asked 'Why, what does your brother want of you?' Richard picked up a flower head that had dropped from the bunch she carried 'He wishes to make a grand funeral for our father and our brother Edmund' Richard looked at his wife rather sadly 'I hardly remember my father or Edmund for I was barely eight years old when the Battle took place at Wakefield and my father had rarely been with us. Edmund was also killed after that battle so I imagine that Edward will wish his remains to be honoured too. I understand his wish to have our family

71

decently interred but he has left it long before making this decision' Richard looked down rather sadly at the flowers 'And why must you go to Court?' his wife asked, 'Can he not do this without you? What of the Scots?'

He drew her down onto one of the little camomile seats and with his arm around her shoulders he explained, 'My love, I have to arrange the whole matter for I am Constable of England and this is one of my duties. The re-interment is to be at Fotheringhay. That was our family home, if I could call anywhere home when I was a young child. I was born there and I do recall a little about it and of being there with my sisters and George. There is to be a family mausoleum and a grand procession and I know not what beside and I must arrange for all these. But I have to have audience with King Edward beforehand.' He was dangling his plain black hat between his knees. His face looked grey. Anne knew that he was both tired from his current duties and sad when he thought of the father of whom he had seen so little.

'Come within, my Richard,' she said, 'and let us speak more of this.' So they went into their chamber and sat together on the seat in a window embrasure. Richard sighed. 'There is no point in speaking much of this' he said 'Edward has decided and I must go. I can leave it until a few more days have passed but then I must ride to meet him at Fotheringhay. It will take time to make the preparations, my Anne, and I mislike to leave you for all my joy is with you and our son. But I am Edward's man heart and soul and fealty for he is my sovereign lord and King as well as my brother.' 'I know that full well and I understand it.' Anne replied. 'And I am glad that we may have a few more days together. Must I attend the reburial?' 'I will know more when I have had speech with the king. Do you still love me, my Anne?' 'How can you ask it!' she was not hurt for she understood her husband. And she told him 'I love you even more than when you came to free me from bondage in that cellar' She smiled at him and laid her small hand in his strong one. He was not a big boned man and he stood no more than five feet and eight inches tall in his boots and his white and delicate hands were not large but yet they were strong. He was well muscled too and she knew that he was a skilful warrior for all his gentleness.

Anne also knew how his difficult childhood had made him reserved with everyone but her. She treasured the fact that with her and with his children he could be so much at ease that he laughed and sang with them and could converse without taking care of every word that he said. The chapel bell rang. 'It is dinner-time my husband let us go to the table.' She said and led the way to the great hall where the whole household ate together. As they ate Anne said 'If you will be near enough, my lord, you might visit Luke' Richard's face lit up. 'That is true! Why, my Lady of Love, you think of everything! It cannot be more than a day's ride!' Anne smiled at him 'Now you see the task is already easier to bear!' He leaned toward her took her hand and kissed it. 'You are the best wife in the world!' he said. Her face blushed just a little and she retorted 'And you, my Richard, are the best husband!'

So three days later Richard rode to London with Master Kendall his secretary and a few of his trusty Yorkshire-men. After his long journey from Middleham he was warmly received by his brother Edward and together they planned the state funeral of their long dead father. 'What of Edmund' asked Richard 'do we include him in these honours?' 'We will inter him at the same time,' said Edward 'but since he was not a duke and was so young we will not include him in all the honours' he noted Richard's doubtful expression 'Never fear,

Diccon, we will do right by our late brother.' 'I hardly knew either him or our father' said Richard. The king said 'You were all so young and we had to keep you safe, you and George and our ladies' Edward sighed. 'it seems so long ago now. How fast time passes!'

So Richard planned a funeral fit for a royal duke. The cavalcade was huge. The late duke's coffined body was laid on a grand and ornate hearse on which it was guarded by a silver angel. The hearse was draped with a black pall on which were the blazons of England and France and a jewelled crown was placed over the head of the coffin to show that the late duke had been of a royal line.

Richard followed his father's hearse for seven long days, riding alone on a black charger with the saddle cloth and harness fittings all of sombre black. He rode from Pontefract where his father and brother had been disinterred and coffined until at last the enormous cortege reached Fotheringhay. There the cavalcade was met at the castle gates by the King and all the greatest nobles of the Realm. Alms were distributed to five thousand needy people that day and some twenty thousand folk had gathered to watch the proceedings. Richard had done all that Edward had asked of him and all that his father's remains and his earthly dignity deserved. And Richard who was the late duke's youngest son was able to return to his beloved wife and son, and to their equally beloved home at Middleham. Richard who set great store by chivalry, blood ties and family loyalty felt that he had done his chivalric duty by his father and his brother and he was content.

Chapter 17.

A Time for Peace, a Time for War.

Richard was always kept busy. The work of keeping the North was unremitting for there were always minor incursions of the Scots across the border into England. And of course there were English raids the other way. Added to which Richard had other State duties and other lands to administer. He was ably served but of necessity he had to visit many people and places and to read many State papers. But he worked quickly and methodically and always tried to spend as much time as possible time at Middleham with Anne and his children who were all growing up fast now!

There were some interesting social occasions in his life: he and Anne had become members of the Guild of Corpus Christi in York and they attended when there were important meetings and grand banquets held by the Guild officials. These were times to dress like a duke and duchess and Richard and Anne never let anyone think that they could not play the part! They wore their finest clothes and were sociable, chatting with the merchants and burgesses as if they were life long friends. Indeed some were friends for Anne's Neville family were always a force to be reckoned with in the North, and many people remembered Richard from his young days in Warwick's household for he had been a serious minded but pleasant and polite young lad.

Richard and Anne were rich now. Lands and honours were almost constantly heaped on the duke by Richard's grateful brother the king. Richard put this wealth to good use as a patron of the local Churches and religious houses and to pay his subordinates to help him keep the peace and run the lands over which he was, under the king, the ruler. There was money left for running his various establishments around the counties and for disbursing alms. Richard also bought books and patronized writers. Nor was he averse to fun, so that mummers and minstrels were welcome in the ducal home especially at feast times like little Edward's birthday or other family occasions. At these times Richard and Anne wore their best and most expensive clothes but ordinarily their habits were more frugal and they were happier to wear quite plain and simple clothing that fitted their busy lives.

The Scots were still troublesome and together with the other Northern lords Richard had always to be on his guard against Scots incursions. But he had managed to organize a truce of five years with the Scottish king so that there was some respite from that particular problem. There were disputes in the Northern lands from time to time and Richard was called upon to settle these. He did this with out fear or favour. Richard and Lady Anne would visit York, from time to time for the celebrations of the Corpus Christi Guild, to which they both belonged, and for other special occasions. Anne sometimes took the opportunity when in the City to do a little shopping, for there were things she needed for herself and r family. The children were all growing fast and needed things that she could not always find at Middleham fair and there were often small items of clothing for Richard, who hardly ever noticed when his were worn out!

On one such foray Richard had also had done some shopping. He visited a goldsmith and purchased a large and beautiful sapphire of which he had heard and he commissioned the smith to set it in a golden frame engraved with holy pictures and with a relic in a locket at the back. It was a gift for his beloved wife.

Apart from visits which he had to make to other nobles and to mayors and the commanders of his garrisons Richard lived with his family. He and Anne were happy and comfortable together and she had the further blessing of her mother's presence. So life was sweet and relatively undisturbed for about four years. Anne sewed and brewed simples from the herbs in the garden and when they visited York from time to time she had the opportunity to make some social calls. Anne also knew that her mother had become a sister of Durham Priory, so Anne followed suit. This was one of her ways of charitable giving. She felt that she had much to be grateful for. And all the time the love between Richard and Anne grew stronger and developed so that they knew each other's very thoughts.

Chapter 18.

Treachery in the Family

The family news in 1477 was terrible. George of Clarence had been suggested by his sister Margaret, now the dowager Duchess of Burgundy, as a husband for Mary of Burgundy the only child and heir of her late father the duke. Clarence's wife Isabel, Anne's only sister, had died giving birth to a boy child who had also died. Margaret thought George would benefit from a new wife and from having somewhere where he could be the ruler, something which would harmlessly fulfil his ambitions for power. This was not to King Edward's liking so that nothing came of the suggestion. George was disappointed for he thought himself both irresistible as a husband and also as a wonderful ruler, although a ruler in-waiting. To make matters worse Edward had suggested his brother-in-law Anthony, Earl Rivers, whom George disliked intensely, as a suitable match for the Burgundian princess.

Clarence snapped. He had Ankarette Twynhoe, his late wife's maid, hauled up for what could only be described as a mockery of a trial on trumped up charges of poisoning his wife. Isabel had actually died of child-bed fever. He also charged a man with poisoning Isabel's baby son, who had not long survived Isabel's own death. He had them both hanged. He thus usurped the King's Justice as well as committing what amounted to murder.

Clarence had not taken into account either the strength or the reach of the queen's Woodville relatives and their influence. Soon Edward's ears were full of his brother's scandalous and treasonable doings. Some tales were probably true and some were exaggerated; others may well have been invented. Then the proudly unrepentant George of Clarence went even further. He had a priest publicly read out a document that suggested that he, George Duke of Clarence, was the rightful king and that he had previously been appointed to reign after the death of Henry VI.

Worse still George had gone on to gather armed men about him and had raised a rebellion. This had not lasted very long but it spelled doom for George. His brother Edward finally became short of patience for this troublesome brother who had already rebelled with the late Earl of Warwick and had been forgiven and reconciled with Edward. Now King Edward had his brother George called before many grandees and the members of Parliament. Edward personally accused his brother of treason and committed him to prison in the Tower of London. The sentence for such treason could obviously only be the death penalty.

Richard and Anne were in the North at their beloved Middleham. As soon as word of this disaster had been brought from London Richard rode as swiftly as he could to the Court in order to beg Edward to spare George's life. Richard had no great love for the Woodvilles the family of the queen for they were promoted everywhere and had somehow managed to force a space between Richard and his brother Edward, one which had never existed before, but he did not hate them as George did. These people had not deliberately made George of Clarence a traitor but his treachery was in part due to his bitterness towards the queen's grasping family.

Luke joined Richard as he rode hard for London. They talked on the way whenever they rested for food and sleep and Richard told Luke of how he and George had been together as children and that although he knew George could be difficult he still loved his brother and was of the opinion that much of what aggravated Edward was poisonous gossip that had been poured into his ears by the queen's relations. 'How can I help to reconcile my brothers?' he asked. Luke who was now a monk and fulfilling his vocation, suggested that he and Richard should pray for peace between the brothers and that they should also pray for Richard to be given the eloquence needed to speak with the king and to persuade him to show mercy. Together the two men went into the nearest church and knelt in urgent prayer. Then they continued their journey.

They went directly to Court where Richard asked for speech with his brother Edward. But for all his eloquence he could not move Ned to pity. 'Diccon!' said King Edward 'I know that you love George and believe me so do I. And I know that you are loyal to me and would never think of treason. But George is not like you, little brother. George is by nature treacherous. He incited men to rise up against me and would have killed me to make himself king. All this you know. I have forgiven George many times for his reckless behaviour and lack of trustworthiness but all to no avail. He is in prison in the Tower of London. I will have to sign a warrant for his execution, but I do not wish to do so at this season, so near to Christmas. Do not ask me again for mercy for our brother for I dare not grant it. My own life would be at risk if I did. I give you leave to visit George should you wish to do so. Your presence may be a comfort to him and he may even be brought to repentance. Should he then accept his guilt, yield to me and make his submission I might yet think again.' That was the most that Richard could manage before he found himself dismissed with a command to send for his wife and son to join in the celebration of Christmas.

Of course Richard visited George of Clarence in his prison. As a duke and a brother of the king George was at least comfortably lodged and well fed but he knew now that he was deep in trouble. Yet always optimistic, he still believed that King Edward would once again pardon him as he had always done before. So he greeted his serious-minded younger brother gaily 'Have you brought me some Yuletide cheer little brother?' he asked. Richard was surprised. 'Why, it is not yet quite the season and I did not think of it!' He was sorry that in his hurry he had brought nothing but his good advice and brotherliness. 'Oh, don't let that concern you! Just send me in some malmsey wine!' said Clarence, laughing.

Richard talked with his brother for some time marvelling at how sure George was of Edward's pity. George obviously did not understand how much he had offended, and so sure was he of his brother's love for him that he was certain that he would soon be free again. 'I have done nothing unpardonable, Diccon, nothing that Ned would not have done himself!' he told Richard. When Richard left, sadly offering George his blessing and good wishes, George told him 'Do not be so solemn, Diccon. Ned won't kill me!'

Edward did not send the command to execute George of Clarence. All through the Christmas celebrations George remained in his prison feeling ever more certain as the days and then the weeks went by that he would surely be safe.

Anne and Richard were both very miserable during their stay at Court. 'What will happen to your brother George?' asked Anne. 'I do not know, my Love' her husband said 'but I fear Edward cannot save him now. The queen and her family have made such bad blood between my brothers and George is so intractable that I believe Ned has no other way out but to order an execution.' 'Let us go home, my Richard. I do not wish to stay here.' Anne was almost in tears. Richard took her in his arms. 'I know, my dearest and I don't want to be here either but I must stay for the king wishes to consult with me. As soon as the feasting is over and my work here is done we will go back to Middleham. I promise you Anne, my Lady of Love!' But first he visited his mother.

Chapter 19.

Richard Visits Lady Cecily.

The king's mother did not much visit the Court and she knew that nothing that she could say would weigh more heavily with Edward than what his relatives-in-law could say to him. She had heard of course that Clarence was in trouble again but she thought, as did he, that Edward would surely show mercy to his own brother.

Lady Cecily greeted Richard with joy. 'My dear son! How it gladdens my heart to see you' she exclaimed 'it seems such a long time since I saw you! Come and take some wine and tell me how matters stand in the North and how your wife and son do. How is my good-daughter Anne, is she any plumper? The poor child was so thin!' 'She is well, my lady Mother, and so is our son.' Richard smiled at his mother's concern, 'Anne will never be very plump, mother, for her bones are so fine. We are happy at Middleham and the air suits us better than the foetid air of London and the Court.'

Lady Cecily sat down, took up her embroidery and asked him 'What is this matter of George? What has that foolish boy done now?' Her youngest son looked sad. 'He has stirred up rebellion against the king and it was once too often. Also I believe that he tried to frighten him in some way. I do not know how or with what, but hard as I tried, Ned could not find it in him to forgive this last foolishness.' He looked away, across the Thames. He recalled how he and George and their little sisters had clung to their mother's skirts in fear for their lives at Ludlow Market Cross. His mother had remained so upright and proud and had so been a steadfast wife. How had she produced the wayward George!

'And what will become of George?' his mother asked. Richard sighed 'He is in the Tower of London. Edward will have him executed but has hesitated to do so at Christmastide,' He was blunt for there was no other way to tell that stalwart woman his mother the news that he knew she had been dreading. 'I begged most earnestly for his life, mother, but Ned was adamant.' he said. 'As soon as we can leave I shall take Anne back to the North where the air is clean and men are more straightforward. I have come to say farewell for the present for I do not know when I can face coming here again. The Court is so corrupt and if I am nearby at Crosby's Place visit it I must or I shall offend Ned.'

Lady Cecily muttered a prayer and crossed herself and Richard saw a tear glint in her eye but she went grimly back to her work. 'George was always hasty and foolish,' she said 'now he will pay dearly for it and what of his young son?' 'Never fear for the lad mother. I will take him into my household where he will be safe with Anne and me. Ned has promised not to confiscate the boy's inheritance. Mother, I must go now for Anne is anxious not to be alone. I will not fail to write to you of family matters.' He promised. 'Well then my son, go with my blessing.' she said and Richard knelt beside his mother's chair and she blessed him, then he kissed her hand and brow and left her to rejoin Anne at Crosby's Place before they could travel home to Middleham. Lady Cecily was left to think quietly of how much she loved this trustworthy youngest son.

Chapter 20.

Death of a Traitor.

On the sixteenth of January in the year of Our Lord 1478 all
George's dreams of forgiveness were dashed. He was tried by
Parliament on charges of treason and it was his brother the king
himself who spoke against him. Edward said that even after
such treachery he would have pardoned his wilful brother yet
again but that Clarence had made no submission to the Throne
and had not admitted his guilt. Edward said that as it stood he,
Edward, had no choice but to condemn his brother of Clarence
to death for treason to the Crown, that Office being higher than
the mere king. Edward then appointed the Duke of
Buckingham to pass sentence of death upon George Duke of
Clarence.
Edward was not a particularly harsh man nor was he a vengeful
king and his heart failed him. He did not sign Clarence's death
warrant. Eventually on the eighteenth of February the Speaker
of the House of Commons went to the bar of the House of
Lords and requested that if the Duke of Clarence was to be
executed this should be done sooner rather than later, and
preferably at once so that the justice of the land may be seen to
be done. So on that same day George of Clarence was informed
that he would be put to death at once. The execution was
private but the duke was allowed the comfort of a priest and he
was offered food if he required it. Then he was executed. Since
no-one of his family or of any standing was present neither of
his brothers ever knew what his last words were. It was said
that he had drunk deep of Richard's gift of his favourite
malmsey wine. Undoubtedly it had comforted him and given

him courage. His body was buried in Tewkesbury Abbey in the vault where his wife Isabel had been laid to rest.

Richard was sickened by George's treasonable doings and also saddened by Edward's intransigence. 'I do not know how a family can so tear itself to pieces!' he told Anne. 'I thank God that we are not a part of these dark deeds. I can only imagine my mother's grief, for although she knew of his weakness and pride yet George was ever her favourite.' Anne put her arms round her husband and tried to comfort him 'Never fear, my Richard, your brother George made his confession and received absolution at the last and will now be in peace.' She told him 'I fear he may be in Purgatory,' said Richard, 'Anne my love, I must make sure that our family is prayed for. I cannot bear to think of my father and my brother Edmund, and now George in Purgatory with all their sins upon them. For I fear George will not have told all to his confessor. I knew him only too well. I shall seek permission to build oratories for all of us!' 'Now that, my dear love is a very good idea!' his wife exclaimed, 'Where shall they be?' 'I will have to settle that with Crown.' said her husband. 'And when I can have that permission, I shall also build a chapel for the peace of all those souls lost at the battle of Towton. For I know it to have been a terrible slaughter and there is no memorial for the men who died that day. They were all Englishmen and they fought in duty to their liege lords. Their Christian souls need to be saved from long years in Purgatory. King Edward has done nothing for them.'

Richard had never referred to his brother in this way before so Anne could understand the depth of his concern for both his brothers and his own misery at their fates.

They were both unhappy even at Crosby's Place away from the Court, and they had not taken part in the celebrations for the wedding of Edward's second son little Richard of York, who was named for the king's brother Richard of Gloucester. Nor had the Duke of Gloucester played any part in the joust held in honour of the tiny bride for he had not been invited to do so although all knew him for a doughty warrior. The queen's family had ousted everyone else but themselves and their hangers-on from favour at Court. Richard felt cut off from Edward and he could not leave soon enough. Yet he remained loyal to the brother to whom he had sworn allegiance, for Edward was the anointed King, whatever else he was.

In a short while a messenger came from the king bringing licences to build colleges at Middleham and at Barnard Castle where priests and choristers would pray and sing psalms for all the family of York in perpetuity and also for the chapel that Richard had requested to build at Towton. Richard guessed from this that Edward already regretted George's death. And he heard it said that from that day onward Edward's usually sunny personality changed and he had became less affable and more grasping.

Richard noticed that Anne was coughing more and he had no doubt that the London air did not suit her. As good as his word, he took Anne carefully back to the home she loved. She was carried in a litter and wrapped in warm furs and Yorkshire wool rugs.

Chapter 21.

Home to Middleham

They got home to Middleham in March and were glad to be in the clean fresh Yorkshire air 'God's Own Country!' Richard said as they rode home through Middleham village at a little after noon. He pointed out a spot not too far from the castle 'There, just over there I will build a College for priests! We shall be prayed for, my Lady of Love, for ever with all the family. God will forgive my brothers and we will all be saved from Hell and damnation!' He turned in his saddle to look back down the village street 'Look how peaceful it is!' He said 'Nothing but the noise from the forge and people working at their trades. This is how our land of England should be! And it should be in this good English which we all understand that laws and judgements should be made not in debased Norman French for we are all English men and women now!' Anne looked at him. His eyes were shining bright blue in their deep sockets and his face was flushed with the exertion of riding. She feared he may have a fever but then she saw tears in his eyes. 'My Richard, she said 'I know that you grieve. Why do you not send for Luke? He will set your mind at rest and it is not so far from here to his friary.' 'I will do so,' her husband smiled at her 'My Anne! You think always of all good things!' They went into their beloved home where at last they could relax.

That night in their great bed Richard took his wife for the first time in many weeks. He had not touched her in all the time that they had been in London. She had begun to think that he no longer loved her and shyly she said so. 'Oh, my dearest, how could you think that?' Richard was appalled 'It was just that in that place – that damnable place - love seemed cheapened. My brother Ned,' he checked himself 'my brother the King has so debased himself that all around him are soiled, Anne, my beloved, and I could not touch you in case I too was soiled by the presence of such lust and debauchery.' He gave a heavy sigh, 'I enjoy the good things in life like fine clothes and good food. And I enjoy seeing you with gems to wear and I love you and you beautiful body. But that is a sacred love. The king makes the act of love something shameful and his pleasures become cruder and less magnificent the more show there is. It is because he has lost his soul Anne.' He sounded so bitter and Anne, who knew him better than any other living being, knew how much Richard suffered. She tried her best to soothe him and at last they slept.

Luke, now Friar Luke, arrived in due time and spoke with his master for a long while. 'You must not blame yourself, my Master Richard of Gloucester,' he told his friend 'your brother George was a foolish man and an ambitious one. He would not have cared too deeply had it been you who was to be killed. For foolish and ambitious men are always selfish. You are not to blame for his evil doings and nor can you be blamed for not succeeding in persuading his Grace the King to reprieve your brother. You did your best. And you are raising colleges of priests to pray for your family and a chapel for those who fell in that terrible fight. Your heart is kind. Your conscience is clear. And you do a fine thing for your king and country here in the North. I hear, even far off in my Friary, of how you maintain peace and justice. Cease to condemn your self. Has it not occurred to you that it may perhaps be a sin not to recognize God's love for you and His forgiveness for your brothers and for all of us?' 'I had not seen matters in that way' replied his friend 'I thank you, Brother Luke! Yet again my friend you have done me great service! Take this when you return to your Order, it is a small offering to your House in recognition of your goodness to me' and he handed Luke a heavy purse.

Luke stayed for a little while longer and Lady Anne also found time to speak privately with him and to ask a question: 'Do you think, Brother Luke that it is perhaps because we had no papal dispensation for our marriage that Richard and I have only one child?' 'I think, my lady, that had that been the case you would have had no child at all.' answered the Friar. 'I believe that God may not have blessed you with little Lord Edward had he been so angry! Are you concerned, my lady, that you have only one child?' Luke looked kindly at Anne's anxious face. 'Yes, I am' she replied simply. 'My lady, if I may make so bold, I believe that it is a combination of your own frail health and your lord's frequent absence that you have not again conceived. Do not disturb yourself, lady, for these things are in God's hands. You have a husband who loves you above all but his God, and you have a beautiful son. Be grateful for those blessings and for Lord Richard's love for you!' 'Bless me, Brother Luke, and pray for me, will you?' 'It is my privilege to pray for you, lady, and I will gladly give you my blessing.'

Luke rode away soon after that and Richard went on with his plans for the colleges at Barnard Castle and Middleham and the Towton chapel. Soon walls were rising and stained glass windows were being commissioned.

Chapter 22.

Lord of the North, Under the King

Richard and Anne lived quietly in their home at Middleham.
Richard worked hard for there was much for him to do as Lord
of the North but he was always glad of his wife's love and
encouragement. 'My Anne! you are my better self!' he told her
one day as the sat together in the evening light. 'What do you
mean, my love?' 'What I say. You are the reason that I live and
work. You and little Edward! I love the king my brother but it
is for you especially that I wish this country to be safe'. He was
grave-faced as he spoke.
Anne guessed that something worried him 'What is troubling
you, Richard?' she asked, 'Why are you so solemn today?' 'I
have news from further along the border. The Scots are making
more forays. It seems that we may find ourselves at war again'
her husband was very solemn and she knew that he was not
sharing all the news that he had with her. She told him 'I will
not pry, my dearest, but if there is more that you are willing to
tell me I will undertake not to speak of it to anyone else.' She
sent an anxious look across at him. 'No, my dear love, there is
nothing else to tell you. The Scots will make more forays for
they are always trying to find a weak spot. They will find one
doubtless, but it will take them much time for I have ensured
that all fortresses from great castles to very small fortifications
are well repaired and strengthened. I have done all that I can do
with the men and means that I have. Yet I fear it will not have
been enough. But you will be safe here, dearest Anne, for they
will not get to Middleham!' 'Are you sure, husband that there
will be an attack?' Anne asked. 'Not entirely but I do believe

that they will try.' He answered. Noting the worry lines between her husband's blue eyes, Anne changed the subject.

War came at last in June of the year of Our Lord 1482. The Scots had gathered an army and raided across the border. This was no small incursion but a serious attack. Richard and his trusty men joined with the Earl of Northumberland and his array to counter-attack. And Richard and Lord Percy together did this in some style.

While her husband was away Anne found herself in total charge of her home. There were plenty of matters to occupy her for it was natural that those who would have consulted the Duke would often consult his Duchess when he was not himself available. Anne did what she could, knowing her husband's fair-minded and merciful dealings with small petitioners and offenders. But she missed him so much! She lay in their great bed alone and lonely. Her cough was even more irritating now and she often felt very tired. It was colder than she could ever remember, but she thought that this might simply be because of the space beside her in the bed. She could have asked her waiting woman to share the bed with her as many ladies did in those days, but she wanted none near her but Richard. The only other reason for her feeling of chill was her own health which she did feel to be declining. She was sure that she would be restored fully when her Beloved returned to her and she prayed daily and nightly for his safety and his return.

And all the while far away and while doing his duty for his brother the king and caring for his troops, planning with the other lords and his officers, organizing reconnaissance parties, and himself taking a manful part in the fighting Richard of Gloucester had in his mind the picture of a slender golden haired lady: the woman who was and always had been the only love of his life. And every day and every night he prayed for her and for their young son, begging God to spare him so that he might defend her and love her as he had always sought to do. He prayed too for those who fell in battle by his hand or by his command for he knew that to take life was a sin, and thus he knew himself to be a sinner although he fought for his Country and his King as the representative of his Country.

He fought also for his own personal honour and that of his Family for he remembered that his father and his oldest brother had given their lives for their belief in their right to reign. His was of an ancient line and he feared to dishonour it. It must not be Richard Plantagenet the duke of Gloucester who was lacking in chivalry! For his own edification he made for himself a prayer and committed it to writing so that he could not forget any words of it.

Richard fought his way to Edinburgh as well as besieging Berwick upon Tweed, a town lost long ago to the Scots. So great was the force that he had gathered and which even included some members of the Woodville family, for the defence of England that the Scots soon decided upon surrender. Because the Scottish king was a slack fighter and lacking in courage his own men turned on him and clapped him into prison. They then made terms with Richard of Gloucester. The town of Berwick-upon-Tweed which Richard and his doughty men had re-taken remained English for ever thereafter. With peace restored Richard set about putting in hand repairing the town of Berwick, but he was anxious to get back to Middleham and his family.

Once Richard knew that all was going well he returned home. King Edward, being pleased and delighted with his brother's success, heaped honours upon him. Richard was not displeased to be given such recognition but he wore his greatness lightly and remained what he had ever been a quiet, thoughtful, serious-minded and essentially a modest, man.

He rode to Middleham, and entered, as he so often did, by the postern gate and silencing the grooms who came to take his mount, White Surrey, went quietly to his own apartments. He could not hear his son Edward chatting and laughing as he played but he saw his beloved Anne sitting by a window and sewing in the good light. He stole softly up to her and kissed the top of her head. She knew at once who was there 'Richard!' she cried, but before she could say more she was coughing. When the fit was over he kissed her 'Will you help me to take off this harness, my Anne?' he asked and quickly she undid the buckles asking questions all the time. 'You cough so much, dearest wife can I persuade you to have our physician attend you?' he had the worry lines between his brows. 'No, my Richard, I only coughed because you took me by surprise and now I am well again and I want to know of your success! You see the news does come here to Middleham!'

Richard took her hand and led her to their favourite seat in the window embrasure where he told of the battles which he had fought and of how doughty his Yorkshire lads were. 'They are wonderful soldiers, steadfast men who remember the rules laid down for them. I would have no pillaging. But, my Lady of Love, I am sad that I had to cause such havoc in the Scottish countryside. I hope that this will never be a necessity again, for we made a good treaty. Berwick is English again now Anne and I hope it will remain so!'

He still looked grave; but then he looked out of the window over the long view of the Wensley Dale that stretched out before them. 'We are so fortunate to live here, my Anne. Here where we both spent childhood years.' Anne nodded, 'Yes,' she said. 'We are. Here where we found our love for each other. Oh, my Richard, my gallant husband, how I love you!' and she laid her head on his chest.

'And I love you, my Anne.' he told her and looking down at her with his deep set blue eyes twinkling, he solemnly said 'But I am a soldier, Wife and at present I am a very hungry one and have ridden many miles with neither food nor drink. Can you help me?' Anne laughed. He was often very funny and always while pretending to be very solemn or severe. Food and wine appeared very quickly for the servants at the postern had warned the cooks that their Master Diccon was back at home. Richard ate and drank more or less in silence for he was truly very hungry and very thirsty and had no time for chatter until he felt less faint with hunger.

Then he washed his hands stretched out his legs and beckoned to Anne to come and sit on his knee. They often sat like this for although he was not a big man she was very dainty, and fitted neatly on his knees and under his chin. He stroked her hair and kissed the top of her head. 'Tell me about our son' he said. Anne told him proudly 'He is out with a groom, riding his little horse on the terrace below! He loves to ride and he wishes that he could ride his father's big grey!' Her husband laughed a little 'He will have to grow faster if he wants to ride White Surrey!' he exclaimed. 'Oh, he is growing,' said the proud mother, then she added sadly, 'I just wish I was growing a brother for him!' Richard sighed. 'Do not fret my love if it is God's will we shall have another child, but you and Edward are family enough for me with John and Katherine too.' Anne smiled up at him 'Katherine is growing fast and she is so pretty! John makes great strides with his practice of arms and they are good and obedient children. I love them both and so does Edward' Richard looked pleased, 'Then I am well blessed to have such a kind wife and good children.' Soon, he thought, my youngest son must begin to learn in earnest his duties as a knight and a lord, responsible to and for his people.

He became serious again. 'I have to report to the Crown. I am told that Kind Edward ails these days. I shall go to London soon for I should speak with him of the campaign we have just completed.' Anne nodded, 'I will not come with you, my Richard, for I have coughed much of late and London air does not suit me. He said 'I know well how the air of both London and the Court both fail to agree with you. Remain here with little Edward, Sweetheart, and I will return as fast as I can. It is hard to be apart from you but I will return as speedily as I can. Edward will not keep me long away from you. You are my whole reason for life, my Anne!'

Chapter 23.

Margaret of Burgundy Visits England.

In the year 1480 Margaret of Burgundy the sister of King Edward and of Richard of Gloucester visited England. It was proper that Richard should visit London for a meeting with the sister whom he had not seen since she went to Burgundy to be married to the duke. That was years ago, and so Richard set off to visit from Middleham to greet her and to enjoy a family reunion.

Margaret and Richard had been at Fotheringhay together in their childhood and both had loved the library in the College of priests there they had both gone on to enjoy the written word and had both since become the patrons of writers.

Margaret had come to England not only to visit her close family and her other relatives but also as an ambassadress for Burgundy her adopted country, in whose political life she had for a long time had a hand and which was now in danger. Margaret was concerned that England which had always been a friend of Burgundy had now made friends with France. Margaret's brother, King Edward had made a shameful treaty at Picquingy which ranged England with France against Burgundy. Margaret urgently hoped to persuade Edward that England should remain the friend of her adopted country.

The welcome arranged for her was suitably grand and she was also able to visit her mother whose presence in her life she sorely missed, and the other remaining members of her family including her brother Richard, to her great delight. He had visited her rooms very quietly and unceremoniously. When her servant announced him he stepped forward almost shyly to greet her. 'Richard!' she exclaimed 'How you have grown up!' he smiled ruefully 'Not as far up as Edward' he said 'he is so tall that I feel like a child beside him' Margaret laughed at that and said 'You are married to sweet Anne Neville and you have a son. Are you happy?' His face brightened 'I am the happiest a man could be' he told her 'My wife is a beautiful woman who is sweet and loving as you well know, for we are close relatives and you knew her in childhood. And our son is a fine boy.' Margaret noted the little lines between his brows 'Does your back still hurt you Diccon?' she asked, dropping back into the old childhood nickname. 'My beloved wife anoints my back and shoulders with salves that she makes from plants. It helps.' he told her. 'The trouble with your spine does not prevent you from being known as the finest commander and warrior in Europe' said Margaret, proudly 'we hear of what you achieve and also of how even-handed a ruler you are, up there in the northern parts. I too am interested in good governance.' 'It makes good sense to be even-handed and just. Men respect that and they deserve good lordship' he said, serious again. 'Such as that which we hear they get from you my brother. Richard I must ask for your help. Can you help me to persuade Edward to be a friend to us in Burgundy? It was to Burgundy that you both came, and George too, when you needed somewhere safe. Can you help us now?' Margaret spoke with great sincerity. 'Edward is his own man.' Richard told her, looking down 'He will listen to me, Margaret, but whether he will act upon what I say is quite another matter. Why do you not befriend the queen or her brother or another one of her family, for there are plenty for you to choose from!' Richard spoke bitterly 'Do you dislike Queen Elizabeth?' asked the duchess. 'I do not dislike her but I have little trust in her. Her many relatives are so rapacious that every crumb that falls from Ned's table goes to them. Oh, he has been generous to me and I do not complain. Indeed I could do with less! But I distrust the queen's family, Margaret, and very often her own motives. You see what our brother is become. He is grossly fat. He is too heavy to ride a horse and he is not forty years of age. He who was so splendid and heroic a commander, so doughty a soldier! Now he is corrupted by too much rich food, easy living and over much wine. It makes me sad, sister'. Richard looked as disappointed as he felt and spoke. Margaret was quiet for a moment. 'I will take your advice, Diccon, and will court the queen and her family for the protection of my own new country and my own new family. It is indeed sad to see Ned so bloated. They say he enjoys too many women.' Said his sister 'He does,' Richard replied. 'Now there is a new beauty to add to his stable. She's a merchant's wife. She is beautiful and said to be kind hearted but she is overt in scandal.' He pursed his lips. 'Do not play the prude, Diccon. I know of your base-born children.' said Margaret. Richard looked at his sister 'Even their mother was Edward's idea' he sighed, 'he said I must grow up and be a man. But they are beautiful and I love them. They were got before I married and I am true to my wife. That is not difficult. Anne is good and sweet and beautiful. The queen is a beautiful woman too, so what can Edward lack?' 'The thrill of the chase now that he can no longer ride out to hunt' Margaret said and looked hopefully at him. 'So you will try to help me, brother? Ned may listen when you have just handed him such a resounding victory.' 'He may. And I will try. But I am going home to my wife, Margaret, just as soon as I have leave to depart! I came only to greet you and to say farewell and wish you God's speed on your homeward journey when you go.' He bent and kissed her cheek noting happily that in spite of the very slight stoop his damaged spine gave him, he was still taller than she was.

On another occasion a little later that year his brother the king required him for consultation. Wearily Richard rode down to Windsor. He was saddened to see how unwell his brother now looked. He was puffy eyed and bloated with a paunch like a prize bull. What was worse was that the whole of Ned's previously sunny nature had changed too. He talked only of money. Richard noticed how he bullied his servitors and was churlish to his courtiers and even to the churchmen to whom he had always previously been charmingly polite. The queen also looked less than happy in spite of her undoubted hold over her husband. She looked as if she might burst into tears several times while Richard was there and he understood why. Her husband was openly lecherous and had very clearly lost interest in her save for her position as his queen. The new woman in Ned's life was beautiful and her face did look kindly, but she allowed the king to fondle her openly where all could see. Richard was disgusted with the king and with his Court and he left as soon as he could.

Chapter 24.

Peace at Middleham.

Anne and Richard were happy. Middleham was their safe refuge from the world and they loved it and each other. They were well served by their household who loved them. They were received with obvious joy wherever they went in the North of England. Anne was known and respected for her beauty and gentleness and Richard for his kindliness fair-mindedness and his justice. Added to that was his reputation as a fine soldier. So there was great respect for these two young people.

There was one great worry that Richard kept to himself and shared only with his old friend Luke. He wrote to ask him if there was, in the library of the Friary, a book of remedies for diseases of the lungs. For Anne's irritating cough was worse. She had always been slender but now she was truly thin. The cough wracked her fragile frame if she exerted herself too much. But she insisted that she was well in health and that it was only a tickle in her throat.

Luke wrote back that he was sending a messenger with two books but that he feared for the wellbeing of Lady Anne. He wrote that in his own opinion she had been damaged by the cold and damp in the cellar years ago and from the miasma that rose from the streets of Southwark. Richard sighed and put the letter away amongst his papers.

Anne was watching from her favourite window as her son learned sword play on the terrace below. So absorbed was she that Richard surprised her when he put his arms around her. He kissed the top of her head and she looked up so that he could kiss her properly. 'I love you, my Anne.' He said 'Will you take this medicine that Luke has suggested? It might help your cough'. He had a little phial of liquid which he offered her 'I will do so if you really think it will help,' she said 'but I dislike all medicines!' 'But I made this one myself from the receipt that Luke gave me' he protested 'please, dearest Anne, for my sake?' and obediently she took the phial 'All of it?' she asked 'Yes, all at once!' he said and Anne drank it and made a face. 'You could have sweetened it with honey!' she protested. He looked shamefaced 'I did not think of it.' he agreed. 'I will do better next time. Forgive me?' She laughed wiped her mouth and raised her face for the kiss that she knew would come.

He lifted her in his arms and carried her to their bed. 'Was that a remedy for my cough or was it some love filtre?' she asked 'Well now, you drank it, my Lady of Love, so you can tell me what its properties are!' her husband said busy removing her gown 'I love you' he said.' 'And I you' said Anne. They lay naked together on the great bed and rejoiced in each others' bodies and the love between them.

After their lovemaking he laid lazily beside her, holding her in his outstretched arm. 'Well, cough medicine or love potion?' he asked. Blushing, she told him 'Both!' and they laughed together like the children they had once been in this happy place. 'I never dreamed I could be so happy! Especially when I was told I had to marry the dreadful Edward of Wales' said Anne nestling close into her husband's side 'Nor I' he replied, 'although I was always determined that I would find some way to marry you. Regretful as I am to say this or even to think it, for I know it is a sin, but I was glad when I heard that his body had been found on Tewkesbury field. It meant that I might yet marry you. And here we are! Oh, my Anne you are all my world!' and he tenderly kissed her. She was silent for a few moments then she asked 'He did die on the field of battle did he not? I have heard tales of murder...I do not think I could bear that' Richard held her even closer. 'No murder my love, nor even execution, but a warrior's death on the field of battle. I believe it is what that lad would have wanted. He was ever bloodthirsty as they say.' 'I did not love him,' said Anne 'and I never laid with him but I am glad his death happened as you say for I think he wished for marriage with me as little as I wished it with him, so I could not hope for any harm to him! Now, my Lord Duke, we must get up and dress for it is the middle of the day and people will be seeking us!'

So they rose up and went out into their castle again knowing that they could return that night to their secret world of love.

And thus their life continued with Anne watching over her husband and her son and Richard doing his duty by his king and the people over whom he himself had lordship, keeping the Kings Peace and the Law. He was now rarely away from his family for long and they felt secure in their way of life. Richard of Gloucester was well loved by the population for he was a just man and a lenient judge and neither avaricious nor bloodthirsty. He cared about the poor and the infirm and the widowed and fatherless and he cared about the very ground on which he and the people lived. For he loved this land, 'God's Own Country' he called it for its beauty and for the sort of people who inhabited it.

The children of Middleham were growing up. John was showing the makings of an excellent horseman and swordsman and was studying military tactics. Katherine was learning the domestic arts and also how to be a gracious lady which was something which came very easily to one so naturally good natured and kindly. Little Edward was growing. He was of a slender build unlike the more robust John but like his father he had a great heart and would always try to do his best. Anne took Luke's cough cure obediently but it did not seem to help much although she insisted that she felt better for taking it.

Chapter 25.

The King is Dead. Long Live the King.

Then one dreadful April day in the year of Our Lord 1443 the shock came. A messenger with his poor horse exhausted and he grey with dust and worn out by his ride came through the Castle gates at Middleham.

Shown immediately into the Duke's presence the man threw aside his cloak 'My lord' he said 'I have letters from London.' 'From the king?' asked Richard 'No, my lord. The King is dead.' and he crossed himself, offering the letters to Richard.

Richard of Gloucester sat down rather suddenly on the chair behind him. 'What did you say?' he asked. The courier looked sadly down at the duke. 'My lord, his Grace the King is dead' and he again offered Richard the letters he held. Now Richard took them. 'I am so sorry.' he said to the messenger, 'You have travelled far and must be tired and hungry. I did not intend such discourtesy. Please go with my man and he will find refreshments for you, and you should rest.' He nodded to the servant who stood white-faced by the door. The man beckoned the courier and they left the chamber. There were several letters all bundled together. This made the packet heavy. Richard sat for a moment hardly daring to breathe. 'I must have misheard' he muttered to himself. 'Ned cannot be dead!' At last and unwillingly, he opened the packet and drew the letters out. He laid them on the table sorting them. One was from the Privy Council and this he read at once. Then he looked at the seals on the others. Selecting the letter sealed by the Duke of Buckingham he read that next. Then he looked at that from Lord Hastings.

It was true. Edward the splendid, the invincible warrior, the golden, beloved older brother, Richard's king, was dead. Dead in a very few days and no man seemed to know what had killed him at the age of forty years and a little. The Privy Council reported a chill got from fishing by the river. Hastings suggested a seizure or stroke but the letter from the Lords of the Privy Council described Edward giving orders about his will before he died so that a seizure or strike seemed unlikely. Buckingham suggested over-eating or perhaps even foul play although he could not substantiate the latter. The deep set blue eyes were bright with tears that a duke may not shed, not even for a beloved brother. The little lines between Richard's brows deepened.

He chewed the side of his mouth then stopped for Anne would scold him for it. He felt as if he would fall through the chair he sat on. He could not imagine Ned not there. 'I cannot believe this. Edward dead! If I stand up, I shall fall down.' he thought. But it was there before him in writing from various persons of stature. He rang the small bell on his table. Usually he did not do this as he preferred to go to find whoever he wished to speak with but at this moment he felt immobilised.

His secretary came to him. 'Kendall, sit down!' he was terse, which was unlike him but Kendall had already heard. 'My Lord Duke' Kendall said sadly 'I have heard the terrible news. May I offer my condolences? Undoubtedly his grace the king is now with the angels.' he offered, 'That is much to be hoped.' His master said 'I need to write letters, my friend, but I need to talk to my lady first. Will you go and ask her to come to me? And please do not let her know this heavy news until I can tell her myself.'

Kendall left him and Richard sat waiting. He almost bit a nail but Anne would not like that either. He fiddled with the seals re-read parts of the letter from the lords of the Council. A chill did seem a very uncertain way by which to die and he thought that he should discuss such matters with a physician. Anne arrived and he managed to stand up. 'My dearest Anne, please come and sit with me' he said. He was unsure of what he wanted to say and she felt his concern. 'Why, Richard, my dearest, what is the matter? Are you unwell? You are looking very pale.' He placed a seat for her next to his own and she sat down. He began, 'Anne, my love, these letters have come from London.' He touched the seals. 'My brother... the king ...my brother...the king.....Anne, Ned is dead!' 'Is this true? What has happened to him?' she sounded incredulous 'No one has written to say that the king ailed!' she exclaimed, and he told her sadly 'No, it was sudden. Some say a chill others say a seizure. My Lord of Buckingham suggests something more sinister but he does not say why he thinks this.' Richard was as near to weeping as he had ever been. Anne looked at her husband. He was so slender and slightly built but so stalwart of heart and mind and a hardened warrior, but now she saw how moved and grieved he was. 'I will summon Luke' she said. Richard gave her a grateful look, 'You are ever mindful of what will help me, my Anne!' She took his hand and for the first time ever it felt cold. 'My dear Love, have no fear, God will keep Edward's soul for he was kindly to the poor,' she began. 'Oh, I know, but Anne, we must go to York at once. Luke can meet us there and we must hold a Funeral Mass, a Requiem, for Ned, and I must swear allegiance to his son, also I must make all the people here do the same. We must work quickly, my Anne, for the news has not been so swift in getting here!' She rose and said 'Then I will begin to give orders. Has the courier been attended to?' He looked gratefully at her and told her 'I sent him off with one of our men to find him food and drink. He will have rested a little now so I will call him in and have speech with him.'

Her husband seemed to have regained some of his usual poise so Anne left him and went to attend to the matters necessary for a journey to York.

The courier came to speak with Richard who by this time was sitting on a bench seat before the fire, for the April weather was chilly in the Yorkshire dales 'Come and sit here with me, my lad' said the duke and the courier did as he was bidden. He had come with messages to Richard of Gloucester a few times before and was used to his friendly and easy ways. 'It is bad news that I brought you, my lord.' He said rather nervously. 'It is the saddest news for many years,' agreed the duke, 'the king my brother was a splendid man, a great leader and a merciful king. May God have mercy on his soul,' and the duke crossed himself as did the courier. He could see real grief in the duke's face and he knew that these two brothers had used to be very close. 'I was not instructed to hasten back, my lord, so I can wait a while, for a day or even two if you wish, for your replies' he told Richard 'I thank you my friend. I will write as soon as I can. This is a heavy matter and I must send letters out to these parts as well as to London so I am grateful for your patience. Are you refreshed?' asked Richard 'I am my lord. Can I be of more use to you?' asked the man 'Yes' said the duke 'Can you tell me what the word is, in the streets in London and thereabouts, with regard to my brother's death?' 'Why, my Lord, we all thought it sudden-like. He had been a little less than well for a while but it was nothing that a man was like to die of. He carried more weight than most, if you will pardon me, my lord, but then there was a big frame on him.' he paused 'No one has murmured of treason?' asked the duke. 'Well, you know how it is in the City, my lord, and at the

108

Court. There are always rumours' the courier spoke slowly and looked nervous. 'What rumours were there about this?' Richard asked. He was alert but still peaceful 'Well, there was the lady he was so fond of, my lord, as I am sure you will know. Men say that the queen had had enough of her, please excuse me, my lord, but you did ask!' 'Yes, I did ask' said Richard. His eyes usually which were usually so blue were dark grey and shone with tears. He looked away so that the man should not see them.' 'I do not think Master Shore's wife would harm the king.' he said. 'No' replied the man, 'but you see, sir, the queen, well a beautiful lady like she is, she got jealous at last, sir, so they say. There are some as think she may have complained to one of those relatives of hers.' Richard could see from the way that he shut his mouth that the man would say nothing more about it. 'Well, I thank you, my friend. Now then off you go to see my steward and he will find you a bed for as long as you stay. Just one thing' he stood up as did the courier and he looked straight into the man's eyes. 'I would be happy if you would not gossip with my servants or tell them more of this matter than they need to know. It will suffice to say that you have brought me news that his grace the king has died. Nothing more. You understand? 'Perfectly, my lord duke' Richard nodded to him to leave and the courier took himself off to find the steward. Richard knew him for a good fellow who could be trusted. He went to find his wife.

Anne was in their chamber overseeing her women who were packing clothes. 'How is it with you, my lord?' she asked dismissing the women with a nod towards the door. Then she went to him and reached up to kiss his cheek and put her arms around him 'I know there is more to this tale and that it gives you great concern' she said and laid her head against his chest and in doing so she noticed that his heart was beating faster than its usual pace. 'What have you heard that you are not telling me?' She was questioning, her eyes troubled. 'Come, Sweetheart,' he told her 'sit down in our window seat'. When they were seated in their favourite place he took one of the letters from his doublet and pointed to a portion of it. 'See here my love, Buckingham tells me that he knows of a plot. He thinks that my brother was in poor health, but that he may have been assisted out of this world. He suspects poison introduced into the potions given to Ned for the chill he had taken. He says that Ned had time to add codicils to his Will, having read through it. So there cannot have been a severe enough seizure or stroke to kill him. I fear that my brother may have been murdered.' Anne was horrified 'But who would do such a thing?' she cried 'All bounty came from the king so who would profit by his death, or be so far in hatred that they would want him dead?'

Richard was silent. As she sat waiting for him to speak Anne saw the strain in his face. The little lines between his brows had deepened. Slowly he spoke 'Anne, my dear love, there is one who may have been bitter enough to want to harm Ned and perhaps even to kill him. There is one who was as near to him as any mortal.' She was horrified 'The queen? His wife?' she asked 'Ned had never been a faithful husband,' Richard said sadly 'He was always a great and notable huntsman and he loved the chase: that seemed to be so in his private life as well. Elizabeth is a beautiful woman and she would have found it strange that she was not enough for him. Especially when he had wooed her so devotedly and violently even, if the tales are true.' 'What tales are those?' Anne asked. Richard was slow to reply to her, then he explained 'Ned was a hot lover, and it has been said that if he lusted after a woman he would even stoop to violence to have her if she resisted him. My brother was not used to being denied anything, all his life. He was always determined to have whatever he wanted. That was what made him great but it was also what caused his health to decline. And it seems that it may have caused his death. Mistress Shore may have been one woman too many for the queen.' he heaved a great sigh. 'We shall not know,' he said 'this side of Eternity. What the truth of this matter is we can but guess.'

Anne wondered for a while about who might wish ill to the king. Then she said very quietly 'I suppose that the queen had only to speak of her unhappiness to one of her own relations for them to feel that they should act, and she has a son to inherit her husband's throne, although I hear that the prince needs a physician constantly with him. Then there is another, Husband, who would wish all your family and affinity away.'

Richard looked surprised 'Of whom do you speak, my Anne?' he asked 'The Lady Margaret' she replied 'She has always wished to be closer to the throne. Indeed she believes her own son should be sitting upon that throne!' Her husband laughed at her. 'Oh! My dearest Love! You cannot believe that a lady as pious as Margaret Beaufort would ever stoop to think such a thing! And her husband is a faithful supporter of our family.' 'When it pleases or is convenient to him,' Anne pointed out. 'He has not always been as reliable as you think and I believe he changes as the wind blows, York to Lancaster and back to York again. So long as he keeps what is his he will not hesitate to change his cap. And his wife is a strong minded lady.'

The duke of Gloucester prepared to go to York with his wife and his children and their servants all of them in mourning garments. Richard had commanded his letters to be sent ahead to the Clergy and all was prepared in York Minster where a funeral service and Requiem Mass were held for the late King Edward IV. After the services Richard had vowed allegiance to

King Edward V and had caused all the nobility the gentry and the commoners gathered there to swear likewise. He had already sent letters to the Privy Council offering his loyalty and allegiance to the new twelve-year old king, and reminding them that in the case of King Edward's death, he was himself named Lord Protector. He had also written to offer his friendship and his help to his sister-in-law Elizabeth now the dowager queen, in mourning for her husband.

Chapter 26.

Plots and More Plots

Richard rode back to Middleham with his family to prepare to go south to Court to take up his new duties as the Lord Protector during the time of young king Edward the Fifth's minority, as was stipulated in the late king's will. But before he was ready to leave he received another messenger.

This time it was from the Duke of Buckingham. The news in Buckingham's letter was disturbing. Richard called his secretary to him 'Kendall, my friend, there news and it is as bad as I can imagine. I must travel to the south at once and I must desire you to accompany me. Can you be ready in a short time?' 'That I can, sir' replied the secretary, 'I will prepare at once. Do we ride to day?' Richard looked through the great glazed window 'No' he said 'the evening is already darkening the sky. It is too late to start out. We will ride early tomorrow. Can you be ready in that time?' Kendall nodded 'Yes, my lord, I can and will be ready. Who will you take with us? I assume that a guard will be needed.' 'My bodyguard will accompany us with ten other armed men' said the duke of Gloucester 'That should be adequate for I anticipate no need for more force. I will see you just after dawn, Kendall. Go and prepare and get some rest. I will alert the guards myself as I will have orders for them. Good evening to you.'

After writing a reply to Buckingham to appoint a meeting place Richard went to Anne's chamber. She was in her usual place but not sewing. She sat quietly looking out over the dale as the evening darkened. As he entered her slender figure was shaken by the now all too familiar cough 'My Anne!' Richard cried out to her 'Have you taken your cough remedy?' 'I have, my dear, but I still cough! I will be well now for it will work soon. Come and tell me what it is that troubles you, for I see that you are full of concern. It cannot all be for my little cough!' She smiled at him and patted the seat in the window beside her, where they always sat to talk together.

He went to her and sat with her his hands dangling between his knees. She saw this and the little furrows deep between his brows and knew that he was indeed troubled. Anne broke the uncomfortable little silence. 'I saw a messenger arrive' she said 'he was wearing a blazon that I recognize, but which I cannot quite call to mind. Do you have more news that troubles you, my Richard?' Her husband sighed. 'Yes, my dearest Love, I do, and because of it I must ride south tomorrow. The messenger brought news from my lord of Buckingham. Anne, there is a plot afoot and I must go and deal with it. One must cut off the head of a serpent lest it bite!' She was shocked 'Who is plotting?' she asked. Richard sighed deeply again before explaining 'It seems that the queen and her family are trying to rush an immediate coronation for the young king Edward and then to appoint his ministers from her affinity in order to rule in his stead, but as if he were himself ruling,' he explained. Anne was concerned now. 'But I understood that the late king had appointed that you should govern as Lord Protector during the minority of his son!' her husband said 'That is what my brother had always told me and it seems that he had laid it down in his Will.' Richard was grave. 'Young Edward is at Ludlow as was right while he was yet Prince of Wales. His tutor and governor there has always been the Earl Rivers, his mother's brother. Now his mother wishes him taken to London with all speed to be crowned with the same speed in order to circumvent my brother's provisions as laid out in his

Will.' His wife looked at him saying 'So that she may be on hand to tell the new little king what to do and ensure that he does it!' Anne understood. 'How soon must you go, my love?' 'I must leave at dawn tomorrow. I will meet with Harry of Buckingham at Northampton with as much haste as we may make. I am sorry, my Anne, to leave you so suddenly but I believe that if this matter is not attended to swiftly there will be chaos in this realm and also that my own position and perhaps even my life, may be in jeopardy.'

He looked sad and worried and her heart was heavy for him and for the fact that they must yet again be parted. Anne knew that her cough was worsening and lately small specs of blood had flecked her hand-kerchief, but she dared not tell her husband this nor did she want to admit, even to herself, that her health was worsening.

'I will make ready all that you need for your journey,' she said, 'and will you take food and drink with you? I can order what you need from the kitchen' Richard shook his head 'No, my dearest, we will stop at nightfall and wherever we are there is bound to be an inn or a religious house nearby, we will be able to find rest and refreshment. I intend not to be long on the road. Don't concern yourself for we will not starve! I am taking a guard with me but I am leaving adequate protection for you and Ned and the other children here. And have no fear, my Lady of Love, I shall return to you as soon as I may. Let us take some supper now, and then we will go to bed.' 'He kissed her and then called a servant to bring them the light meal of bread and cold meat and light wine that they usually took in the evening. Anne gave instructions for her husband's needs on his journey and at an early hour they retired to bed.

In their great bed Richard took his wife in his arms very gently feeling that she had become even more slender and they made love with their usual sensitive and gentle passion. But even then he had to hold her as a fit of coughing shook her whole body 'Oh, my dear wife! What shall I do to help you? While I am in the south I shall consult doctors of medicine from London to find one who can help you!' 'I will visit the shrine of Saint William in York and beg for a miracle,' said Anne 'perhaps I may conceive another child, too. I have saved up some rich cloth which I have embroidered and I will offer it as a frontal for the altar. I may be blessed!' Anne sounded hopeful and Richard silently praised her fortitude while he grieved for the decline in her health.

Next day he rose at dawn and kissing the golden hair of Anne's sleeping head, Richard rode for Northampton and his meeting with Buckingham.

Chapter 27.

Conducting the New King to London

Richard had not wanted to cause Anne more concern than need be but he had seen from Buckingham's letter that Rivers intended to set out with two thousand men at arms to protect young Edward on the way to London. This sounded to Richard like an army rather than an escort and he smelled trouble.

They made good time. Riding hard and changing horses along the way, he and Kendall and half a dozen men at arms were well ahead of the rest of his party. He was glad to be thinking about the horse and the road rather than what lay ahead. They had stopped on the way only when it became too dark to see properly. Saddle sore and hungry they had put up at any inn that they found and sometimes had availed themselves of the hospitality of religious houses. With the haste they made they met with Harry of Buckingham in just a little more than four days. They found Buckingham's party near to Northampton on the twenty-ninth day of April and Richard felt he would be glad to dismount to stretch his legs and ease his aching back.

Buckingham greeted him in a friendly fashion although they were never previously close friends. 'Greetings, my lord of Gloucester, it is good to see you!' he cried as he watched Richard and his little party arrive. Richard dismounted and extended his hand 'And my greetings to you, my lord of Buckingham! I thank you for your courtesy in sending me warning of these deep matters and in meeting me here.' Richard said. Buckingham gestured towards a sturdy building only some twenty or thirty paces away. 'Shall we go to the inn nearby? There is a good room where we may speak privately.'

'Willingly, my lord' Richard agreed and he added 'have you been here long enough to know if they cook well? My belly tells me it is past dinner time!' Buckingham laughed 'And my guts agree with yours, my lord! And yes I arrived yesterday late in the evening and put up here. My men are all lodged around and about and my sergeant can direct your followers to lodgings if you agree. And I can tell you that the fare here is plain but well cooked and neatly served'. 'In that case,' said the duke of Gloucester, 'I am happy to remain. My secretary is with me and he must also have a room here for I cannot manage without him.'

Together they went to the inn. Master Kendall with his satchel of papers followed them. Inside Buckingham spoke to the innkeeper and he and Richard of Gloucester went up the stairs to a private room which was handsomely panelled and well furnished and with a good fire burning. The two men sat together on a bench seat before the hearth. They were glad of the warmth for the April air was chill. They waited until a servant had brought wine, bread and cold meats for them. When they were alone Richard said 'Well, Harry of Buckingham, what more news do you have for me? This seems to be a bad business. Can you enlighten me?' Buckingham stretched his legs and crossed them at the ankles. He put down his wine cup and looked into the fire. 'King Edward died rather suddenly' he began, 'as you know. I was worried by so swift a death, and then worse still, the queen arranged for a coronation in early May. The new young king was still at Ludlow and so far as I am aware he did not even know that his father had died. The queen called the lords of the Council together and made it clear that young Edward would, while young, rule in name only and that the real power would be with her and her family.' Richard mused 'There are a great many members of her family!' he remarked. 'Where is his grace the new king now? I had thought to meet with him here.' Buckingham was still staring into the fire. He said 'He is at Stony Stratford some ten miles from here where his Woodville relations have placed him. They said that this place was 'too small' for their train of followers!' He looked up directly at Richard 'My lord of Gloucester I believe that they intend to prevent you from being the Lord Protector of the King and this country if they possibly can. I doubt your life is safe with them.' Richard was not surprised 'Ah, so that is the game then' he said 'Well, my lord, you have given me fair warning and I thank you. I would not have come south so quickly had it not been for your letters.'

'We have not always been friends, Richard of Gloucester but we have never been enemies,' said Harry of Buckingham, 'and I see that it would be a sad thing for England if the Woodvilles were to reign.' 'Then what shall we do next,' wondered Richard. He said 'I have held a funeral service for my late brother and I have sworn loyalty to the new king, my nephew, and have offered my service to the queen in her widowhood, but I do not like the idea of a Woodville reign any more than you do.' 'Which is why I have been busy seeking' said Buckingham 'and my servants have found out that Lord Rivers, who has accompanied young Edward from Ludlow along with the queen's son Richard Grey and Sir Thomas Vaughan and a few other retainers, have plans. They are determined to ensure that you do not reach London.' He placed a small packet on the bench between himself and Richard. 'I do have proof should you care to read it!' Richard shook his head, 'No need, my lord, it is as I have already surmised. My only question now is how to elude these men.'

Buckingham gave a short laugh 'I have invited Rivers here to sup with us and to enjoy an evening with us! He has agreed and

I expect that he will arrive shortly'. His companion nodded 'Well done my lord. We will see how the land lies then.' Richard took a sip of wine. 'Rivers is a gentleman and I cannot believe that he would commit any mean or treacherous act.' he said.. Buckingham gave a bitter grunt 'He is dependant on his sister for his position now. Before this he had the protection of the king because they were friends, King Edward, Rivers and my lord Hastings Although Rivers is of a finer grain than either – may God rest the king's soul! But now Elizabeth rules and Rivers must dance to her tune.' 'And that includes the tune 'Stop Diccon?'' Richard remarked looking grim. He then said 'If my brother's last Will and Testament made me Protector during his son's minority then that is the task that I will perform. I owed him my loyalty in his life and that loyalty binds me still, even after his death.' His companion smiled 'Your loyalty, my lord, was never in doubt! Let us see how Rivers acts with us' he said 'then we can decide what must be done. But it is here in writing Gloucester that you must not be allowed to enter London. How will they stop you? Why, man, with a knife in the back!'

If Richard was shocked he tried hard to hide it. He did not ever show his feelings except to his immediate family and his beloved wife - whom, he devoutly wished was beside him now. Then he was immediately glad that she was not; the thought of Anne in any danger appalled him.

He stood up and went to the window looking out onto the fair April countryside. He turned and looked at the man by the fire and the bundle of letters on the bench and slowly he said 'If all that you tell me is true then we are dealing with black treachery here. And for that there is only one answer. We will entertain Rivers and watch him carefully. I will alert my men to keep watch and do you do the same with yours for it might be that we shall need them. But our guards should be hidden so that nothing is suspected. How many men did Rivers bring with him? I read that it was to be two thousand.' 'That was the original number,' agreed the other 'and more like an army than an escort for they have carts full of armaments following behind them. But I did manage to persuade the queen that so many marching men would unsettle the country. I believe that their party is now about four hundred strong.' 'Very well, we shall see what happens,' said Gloucester. 'You have done well; you have I think saved my life my lord and I thank you for your vigilance' He strode across to shake Buckingham's hand. 'Not only your life, Gloucester. My own life would be in danger, too. I am also of the old Royal blood of the land!' Richard nodded agreement then he asked 'What of Grey and Vaughan?' 'They are to stay with the King at Stony Stratford', said Buckingham 'I did not invite the whole party for fear they would bring their escort as well.' Richard of Gloucester nodded his approval.

The two men spent the afternoon quietly. Richard studied the letters that Buckingham had brought with growing discomfort. He wished with all his heart that he was back at Middleham, at peace with his beloved Anne. Buckingham also had letters to read and both men were glad to rest after their long journeys so that there was little conversation. Then as the day wore on Richard looked up. 'At what time may we expect this guest whom you have invited, my lord?' 'I invited him to spend the evening with us to sup and to stay the night here should he wish. I have reserved rooms in the other hostelry nearby. You may have noticed it on your way, here – it is newer than is this house and brightly signposted!' The duke of Gloucester had seen the other inn and nodded agreement. He thought about Earl Rivers. Anthony Woodville was a cultured and studious man with a friendly personality although usually quiet. He was renowned as a great jouster and a chivalrous knight and Richard had always liked him better than the other Woodvilles. He did not know or like Richard Grey so well and he was cautious about Thomas Vaughan, young Edward's chaplain, whose character he did not know at all. But they could wait until the morrow.

As evening closed in, but with the day still bright in the western sky, the earl Rivers rode in through the inn gate. Richard of Gloucester and Harry of Buckingham stood up to greet him as the landlord showed him into the room. They all greeted each other in the usual formal and courteous way of the times. Then Buckingham invited Rivers to sit with them at the table which had been set for supper. Rivers was a tallish man of pleasant appearance and quietly spoken. He was famously scholarly and loved all the arts, enjoying the finest things in life. This evening he was dressed in the latest fashion perfectly tailored and in the best taste. Rivers was courteous and Richard found it hard to believe that this gentleman would be party to any treachery: and yet he had seen proof of it! 'My Lord Rivers,' Richard said with his usual slightly puzzled looking smile, 'may I pour some wine for you? Supper is being prepared and will be here shortly.' Rivers accepted the wine 'I thank you both, gentlemen, for your hospitality. You are most kind' said Rivers and he raised his wine cup in a toast, 'to you my lords and to our new King Edward!' Richard and Buckingham followed suit saying 'To the King!'

A knock at the door announced the arrival of their supper. Buckingham had ordered the best available and it was indeed a veritable feast. They ate and drank and talked of the latest books and discussed the newest music and who was about to marry and whose son and heir had been born. They asked courteously about each of their wives and the harvests that last autumn had produced and even the latest fashions in dress. They talked of everything in fact, except the politics of the day. The evening went well and was convivial. There was a great consumption of wine and Richard, who was abstemious as always, noted how often Buckingham refilled the cup that Rivers drank from. And eventually the earl referred to the new king and how much his mother was looking forward to his reign and how she would be so close to him that no one could give him better advice. Realizing immediately that he had made a mistake he quickly added 'With your permission and guidance, of course, my lord of Gloucester!' Richard nodded 'Aye my lord, with my permission and guidance!'

He had noted the slight slur in the earl's speech. He looked across to Buckingham who very slightly inclined his head before saying, 'Well, my lords, the cock will be crowing in a very few hours! Lord Rivers, my man will see you to your lodging and will attend on you. I bid you a good night, my lord, sleep well!' and opening the door he called softly and one of his own servants came and offered an arm to Rivers who was glad of the support. He bowed to his two hosts and offering rather slurred thanks he bade them a good night.

Buckingham looked at Gloucester 'Well, he made his slip' he said 'and as you saw from the letters that I showed you there are treacherous plans made.' Richard shook his head 'I see that you are right, Buckingham, but I would not have believed this of Rivers had I not seen the proof!' 'What do you intend to do?' asked his companion.

Richard who had been a military man all his life was used to making swift decisions: 'I see no option but to arrest him at dawn to morrow' he aid 'and then we should proceed as fast as we may to the King at Stony Stratford. I will have arrest made of Grey and Vaughan and any others of note, so that no further mischief can be plotted. Not by them, in any case! I mislike to do this, my friend, but I see no other course open to us.' said Richard sadly and he shook his head gloomily repeating 'I would never have believed Rivers to be so base!' Buckingham gave a short laugh, 'Ah, but you forget my lord of Gloucester: Rivers is a Woodville! They are not of good blood, in spite of the duchess Jacquetta's family! They are greedy and they are desperate to ensure their position and their rank and wealth. There is one other matter which was not in the letters which I have shown you. I have been unwilling to tell you of it until now and it is this: Edward Woodville has taken the fleet to sea.' 'He is under me, the admiral, and I have been busy in the north.' said Richard 'So he is,' replied Buckingham, 'but with him sailed your brother Edward's treasury!' Richard was visibly shocked 'However does he expect us to finance England! Edward had garnered as much as he could from all quarters to provide for his government!' 'As I have said, they are greedy, grasping and dangerous! The whole family are of the same mould' Buckingham said, his anger was obvious. 'Tomorrow at dawn, we strike a blow for England!' said Richard of Gloucester. Before he went to his bed he had sent men to Stony Stratford with orders for the dawn of day.

On the thirtieth day of April the Dukes of Gloucester and Buckingham attended on the earl Rivers and politely arrested him. The only surprise that he showed was that they had not done so the previous night. Richard of Gloucester informed him that he had not been in possession of all the facts at that time, but that he knew now knew them. He then turned on his heel and walked to his mount. 'Conduct the lord Rivers to Pontefract,' he told his men 'keep him straightly but treat him honourably for he is an English gentleman.' Without looking at

Rivers and without another word Richard mounted and turned his horse's head to the road. Buckingham followed. 'One down, my lord of Gloucester, and two, or maybe more to go!' he said. They rode more or less silently for the ten miles to where the young king was for they were in haste and there was little more to say. Richard was sadly perplexed to think that such a man as Rivers would be so base.

Arriving at Stony Stratford they at once made certain that Richard's orders had been obeyed and that Grey and Vaughan and the others had been secured and their men-at-arms dismissed. The carts full of armaments had been taken into the custody of the duke of Gloucester's men and it was his servants who now served Edward the new king. Having seen that all this had been done as they had directed Buckingham and Gloucester went to speak with the king.

Young Edward was less than pleased to see them. He had been brought up principally by Lord Rivers to be very aware of his royal rank and very much attached to his mother's family. He hardly knew his uncle Richard of Gloucester who lived mostly in the North and rarely came to Court. In any case as young Edward had enjoyed his own household at Ludlow for several years so he barely knew Buckingham either.

He greeted these other kinsmen coldly. 'Where is lord Rivers?' he asked, 'And where are Lord Grey and Sir William Vaughan?' 'Your majesty's relatives and Sir William are our guests and are on their way to Pontefract.' Buckingham told him. The lad was angry and Richard realized that he was also frightened. He had himself known fear at a young age and so he felt for this lad who was but twelve years old or so, and was left with no one whom he knew well about him. 'Do not fear your Grace,' he said 'they are unharmed and my men have orders to treat them as noblemen deserve. My lord of

Buckingham and I will escort you to London and all will be well.' 'My lady mother, the queen, appointed these men to be my guardians and counsellors and I trust both her and them.' said young Edward. Richard spoke gently 'Indeed, so she may have done but his grace the king, your late father, appointed me to do so and to be Protector of you and your realm until you are of age. My lord Buckingham and I have reason to believe that this should be our concern and that your Grace will be safer with us.'

Edward was not happy and it took some long time to convince him that all was well and that the duke of Gloucester his uncle and the duke of Buckingham his kinsman were there to care for him and to see him crowned. So that night Buckingham and Gloucester had a different guest. They entertained the young king Edward. When they had supped they both spent time helping him to write his new name and title while the two dukes wrote theirs as examples. And because the lad was so nervous Richard also wrote his own motto for the boy to see 'Loyauté me Lie' 'Loyalty binds me' he said 'this has been my watchword ever since I was a young man and was bound to serve your father the late king my brother. And that same loyalty will bind me to you, now that you are my king.' said Richard. Next day they set out for London.

Richard knew that young Edward had only recently been informed of the death of that magnificent man, his father, and was still in grief and that he must also be feeling somewhat daunted by the prospect of his own kingship coming so much sooner than he could have expected. Richard tried his best to cheer the lad and to make him comfortable wherever they stopped along the way. After all this young Edward was very little older than his own young son Edward. He also made time to write to Anne, assuring her of his safety and of his love for her.

On the fourth day of May, in the year of Our Lord 1483 King Edward, the fifth of that name was escorted into London by the dukes of Buckingham and Gloucester. Richard was privily informed that the royal apartments at the palace at Whitehall were not in a fit state to receive the king because his mother had stripped the furnishings out and had taken them with her to sanctuary in Westminster under the protection of the Church. The Abbot's dwelling had had to have a wall knocked down in order to allow access for all her goods and chattels. Knowing this Richard conducted the king to the Bishop's palace at St. Paul's and it was there that young Edward received the oaths of fealty of the lords temporal and spiritual. Edward was comfortably installed and soon settled into his new role as king.

By the tenth of the month Richard was able to call a meeting of the Council during which his position as Protector was confirmed and the coronation which young Edward's mother had planned to take place immediately was re-scheduled for the twenty second day of June, this to be followed by the first Parliament of his reign which was to be called for the twenty-fifth. As the Protector Richard now confiscated many Woodville lands in order to lessen the family's power base. The Duke of Buckingham was richly rewarded for his assistance in preventing the lately intended coup. Other than that Richard made few changes to the administration set up by his brother, the late king. Everyone settled down to prepare for the coronation. Elizabeth, widow of the late king refused to come out of sanctuary and kept her daughters and her second son with her. Lord Stanley remained as steward of the royal household. He was the fourth husband of Lady Margaret

Beaufort whose son Henry Tudor was living in largely self-imposed exile in Brittany. Richard thought it sensible to keep his lordship close where he could more easily watch the step-father of Henry Tudor.

Chapter 28.

Anne Awaits News

Anne was happy at Middleham, amongst the family and friends whom she loved, but she missed Richard and especially at night when she was alone in their great bed. Sometimes now that the weather was a little warmer, she had the hangings over the window of the bedchamber drawn back and the shutter opened. She coughed less then and it was also good to have a view of the beautiful dale spread out before her. The cough was getting worse now and in fact it was quite a nuisance. She was finding it harder to hide how it wracked her body. She was losing so much weight that her sewing woman had taken in all her gowns. But although she tried to eat a little more she found that her appetite was poor. She told herself that of course this was because Richard was away. She was sure that as soon as they were together again she would recover 'You will need to let my seams out again as soon as my lord comes home!' she joked to her serving woman.' 'Yes, my lady, so I will!' said the woman but inwardly she felt sad. She had been Anne's servant for years now and knew her all too well. She passed a clean kerchief to her mistress and took away the blood spotted one that Anne had used. She was shaking her head as she went from the room.

There was a more cheerful event the next day for there was a letter from Richard. Anne took it to their chamber and read avidly. He had written of the events at Northampton and Stony Stratford but he had not given names in case anyone else should see the letter before it reached his wife, but Anne understood at once for she well knew who was involved. She was concerned for Richard but she knew that he was sensible and had taken reliable men with him. At the end of the letter was his personal message of love to her. This she read and reread over and over for the only things about which she truly cared deeply were her husband, his well being, their son, and the love that was between them.

While Richard was away there was the usual stream of requests, petitions and complaints that he would normally have dealt with but which, in his absence, people brought to the duchess for attention, as his nearest representative. Anne did the best job that she could, always thinking of what Richard would do in any circumstance and with the help of Thomas the assistant to Master Kendall, she usually found that she could satisfy the people who addressed her. But she was so tired! Between coughing and her lack of Richard there were days when she could only leave her bed with much effort and self discipline. She wrote to Richard but she did not tell him of her illness. However she did send a message to Friar Luke to ask him if he could send a stronger remedy for her cough.

Before she received a reply she had further news from her husband. A courier came galloping in through the castle gate. He was covered in dust and crying out urgently that he came from Lord Richard and must have speech with the Lady Anne. Servants brought him to her solar. Taking one look at the man she called for ale for he was clearly thirsty. 'Drink, my good man and then tell me your message' Anne said with her usual gentle kindness. Gratefully the rider quenched his thirst and then he said 'My lady, my lord the duke has commissioned me to bring you to London. He wishes for your company and asks that you come with as much haste as you may, so that you do not become discomforted. All is well with him. He sends you a token.' He reached into the inside of his doublet and brought out a small package. Anne took it, her fingers eagerly tearing at the wrappings. It was the gold ring with two small diamonds side by side that Richard usually wore on his little finger. This ring she given to him at their marriage. It had belonged to her and so of course it was too small for any other of his fingers. Around it was a scrap of parchment on which his neat script told her that she might trust the man who brought it to her.

'How soon does my lord wish us to leave for London?' Anne asked the messenger. 'I believe, my lady that my lord wishes you to set out as soon as it is convenient for you to do so. There are many things afoot in London, Lady, and his grace the duke needs you with him'. 'Very well.' said Anne 'We shall prepare quickly and depart tomorrow or the next day at the latest.' Anne had made up her mind and she quickly organized her household. She made sure that the children were all well and had everything needful to their welfare and she knew that her household servants could be trusted to keep everything running smoothly in her absence. She arranged with young Thomas that he would send on any correspondence to the duke's house in London and that he would deal with anything with which the steward needed help. Then attended by two of her ladies and a small contingent of her husband's men-at-arms she prepared to travel to London to rejoin her beloved husband.

She found riding too tiring now and so she travelled in a litter. The head groom at Middleham had found two well matched and sensible horses in order that his lady would not be too much shaken about. Anne was a sweet and gentle soul who was much loved by those who served and knew her, and her comfort was important to them.. Anne's baggage travelled behind on sumpter mules and her ladies rode but took turns in keeping their mistress company in the litter.

They travelled as fast as they could but even so it took a full week to reach London. Anne had sent ahead to her good-mother, the lady Cecily, to announce her arrival for she was not sure where Richard would be staying, and she wrote to Friar Luke to advise him that she would be travelling to London and to ask that any remedies be sent to Baynard's Castle.

Although she was worried about the reasons for her husband's summons to her she was never–the-less delighted to be on her way to see him.

Chapter 29.

A Fatal Meeting.

Matters proceeded in a regular fashion in London, for Richard was well used to maintaining order and was well liked by those who knew him. Sadly most of the people of the south knew only of his deeds, and not of his personality, and they found him very different from the magnificent and flamboyant King Edward the Fourth. Richard was much more retiring and controlled, and he did not carouse in public places or womanize amongst the courtiers' ladies or the merchants' wives.

However folk soon found him to be just, fair-minded and merciful. They were glad that he would bring the little king up and teach him to be like himself.

There was to be a meeting of the Council on the thirteenth day of May. On the twelfth day of May a servant waited on Richard with a note from Buckingham. Looking up from it Richard said. 'Please inform his lordship that I will see him now.' He had no feeling of concern for he and Harry of Buckingham had been working together ever since they had met at Northampton. He was sure that this would only be some small matter that needed his attention, so he went on reading the book that he had picked up when seeking a few minutes of pleasant diversion.

A knock on his chamber door announced the duke. 'Come in, my lord!' Richard welcomed the duke with his usual puzzled looking smile, 'How may I help you this fine day?' 'A good day to you, my lord Protector' said Buckingham 'and may you be protected!' he looked worried, a frown deeply marking his features 'Why, man, what is the matter that you come with such a dark countenance?' asked Gloucester. He gestured to a seat, poured a cup of wine for the duke and laid his book away. Buckingham drank a little and then he said sadly 'Richard of Gloucester, I have news of a plot.' He took a sheaf of letters from his pouch. 'There is a scheme afoot to oust you and in fact to kill you.' 'There is nothing so very new then! Who is it this time?' Richard said, for he was getting used to London ways. Buckingham shook his head 'The principals I know of but there may be others. Lord Hastings has been conspiring with Archbishop Rotherham and with Lord Stanley and Morton the bishop of Ely, and also with the queen. The plan is to waylay you at the Council meeting tomorrow and to make certain that you do not survive so that they may regain control of the king and the country.' Richard was silent for a few moments. Then he said 'I do not intend to throw this country to the dogs, Buckingham, but show me proof.'

Buckingham stood up and laid his letters open on the table. 'Read these. I have received them this morning from my watchers' 'You spies?' asked Richard. 'If you wish' rejoined the Duke. 'I have to watch my own back, Gloucester, as well as yours. I also descend from King Edward the Third and am just as much persona non grata as you are, where the Woodvilles and their friends are concerned'. Richard began to read. He read carefully but was clearly angered by what he read 'This is such blatant treason!' he exclaimed 'Can they not see that this country is not such as to be ruled by a woman! English men are the best in the world but they are in need of a strong arm to rule them or their very courage leads them astray! And besides this is contrary to my brother's Will.' He turned to Buckingham saying 'My lord, we must act fast for this canker will spread if not felled at once!' 'What do you intend, for you will not go to the Tower to meet the Council tomorrow?' asked Buckingham. 'Oh, I shall go and so will my guard!' Richard sounded determined. 'I have had enough meddling from that sorceress the queen! As for the others, Hastings led my brother from greatness to debauchery and death and the clerics are no doubt lining their purses. Stanley was ever a turncoat, but he is also a good administrator. I shall deal with them.' Buckingham nodded. 'It is well that you should' he said. 'I will see you tomorrow in Council. Good day to you my lord and I pray Heaven will preserve you.' He bowed, as did Richard and left the room. Richard turned to the pile of papers on the table carefully dealing with each one in turn.

Chapter 30.

Another Crisis.

Just after dinner Richard had another visitor. This time it was
Bishop Robert Stillington. Richard bade him welcome and saw
him to a seat and poured wine for him 'What is your business
with me, Father?' Richard had heard of this cleric but had not
previously met him. The priest looked worried. 'My lord of
Gloucester I come on a difficult and delicate errand.' Richard
nodded and drew up a stool to seat himself before this man of
God. 'Please tell me very simply what it is that you look so
worried and care-worn about. I will help if I can.' He eyes were
kindly and he was smiling his shy smile His voice was warm
and encouraging. Robert Stillington was still uncomfortable but
felt a little more courageous from the wine.
'My lord, it is about the late king, your brother' began the
cleric 'I have long kept as a secret something that I should
perhaps not have kept hidden. But yet it seemed to me to be
best to remain silent.' Richard was puzzled and wondered what
the man could possibly be talking about. Edward had always
deferred to the clergy and had never defiled a church or
committed any sacrilege that he knew of. 'Go on, Father'
Richard said. Stillington took a deep breath. 'My lord, in the
year of our Lord 1460 I married your brother Edward then still
Earl of March and about to become king, to a great lady.' 'In
the year 1460 you say?' said Richard who was now completely
bewildered, 'But Father, my brother was married to the queen
in the year 1464 although it was at first a secret, and they were
wed for many years, near nineteen in all, until he died' 'The
great lady to whom I joined your brother in matrimony was not

lady Elizabeth Grey' said the priest and his eyes were downcast. 'I married Edward of March to the Lady Eleanor Talbot. There were just the three of us present. So you will have to accept my word.' Richard was worried. He stood up and walked about the room biting his under-lip. 'Father, are you sure?' he said at last. 'My son, I am absolutely certain, and I will testify to any man, in any place, that I speak the truth.' He looked very solemn. 'My lord duke, the late king's marriage to lady Elizabeth Grey was and is bigamous.'

Richard looked hard at the man and his eyes were now piercingly blue, 'So, Father, whom else have you told or spoken to of this?'

Stillington looked down at his hands and fiddled with his Episcopal ring, 'I was asked to offer spiritual comfort to your brother of Clarence when we both happened to be guests of the Crown at the Tower of London,' he explained 'The duke of Clarence enjoyed some wine, my lord, and invited me to join him. I fear I may have taken a cup too many and I spoke of the marriage to him at that time. A great sin on my part and one of which I have often repented'. The poor man looked inconsolable.

Richard was thoughtful. 'Was the marriage to Lady Eleanor a true marriage?' he asked 'Indeed it was, my lord,' said the bishop 'And it was consummated to my certain knowledge I being the house priest at that time They remained together for some long time. But when the king your brother took another lady to his bed, the lady Eleanor was very sad as well as shocked. She was a pious lady, my lord, and after that she refused to sleep with the king. I believe that she expected to be publicly recognized and when she was not and he took a mistress she began to have doubts.' 'As well she might!' exclaimed Richard 'I recall something of this' he said 'I think

she was a tall and stately lady of great presence and beauty.'
'So she was, and of a high rank,' Stillington said 'the late king dowered her with many lands and when he made public his marriage to the Lady Grey, the Lady Eleanor became attached to Corpus Christi College in Cambridge, and later while she lived at her manor of Kenninghall in Norfolk she became attached to the nunnery of Mount Carmel. While she did not make a profession, and indeed being married and that marriage being still valid in the sight of God she could not profess, she otherwise lived as a nun. She has since died' He fell silent.
'Poor lady!' murmured Richard. His chivalrous heart went out in pity to the woman whom his brother Edward, the magnificent, had so wronged. In his heart Richard knew the story to be true for while they were in exile together Edward had often boasted to him of how many women he had bedded, and how he had never accepted a refusal.
'So the queen was not my brother's true wife?' he asked 'How could she be, my lord, when the lady Eleanor was alive at the time of her marriage to king Edward?' said the bishop 'And I do not think that there was a further marriage between lady Elizabeth and the king, even when he knew of the lady Eleanor's death' the bishop said. He looked more calmly at Richard now and he said 'I had to tell you of this matter now, my lord, because of the coronation.' 'Why, what of the coronation?' asked Gloucester. Stillington almost clicked his tongue 'Do you not see, my lord? King Edward's children with the lady Elizabeth are base born. How can we crown his bastard son?' Richard's face drained of colour. 'Oh Loved be God!' he exclaimed crossing himself, 'What shall we do now!' 'My advice is that we put these facts before the lords of the Council.' said the priest.

And so it was that together Richard and Bishop Stillington told the assembled great lords of this matter. The decision was made to discuss the king's marriages in Parliament. But before that, Richard had to be present at the Council meeting, in the tower.

Chapter 31.

More Treachery.

Early the next morning some of Richard's picked men at arms were carefully stationed in a room beside the council chamber and a signal had been arranged. When they heard Richard call out 'Treachery' they were to go into the chamber and arrest certain persons.

The lords arrived. Richard came into the council chamber a few minutes after them. When they had greeted each other and were seated and the meeting had begun Richard asked the lords to excuse him. He left the room and at once one of his men came to him and placed a letter in his hand. Reading it Richard swore. Which was unusual for him, 'By God's Bones!' he cried, 'there has been enough treachery!'

He went back to the council chamber and with him went several of his men at arms. He declared 'Lord Hastings, Lord Stanley, my lord Bishop Morton and my lord Archbishop Rotherham! You are all under arrest on the grounds of your treasonable conduct. You have conspired with the widow of my brother the late king not only to change his appointments made in his last Will but also to murder both the Duke of Buckingham and me. Guards! Arrest these men!' His men took the lords whom Richard had indicated and removed them from the chamber.

Richard read the letter which had been handed to him to the other lords who were still present and now very surprised. It had been written by Hastings and was addressed to the queen assuring her that neither the duke of Gloucester nor the duke of Buckingham would leave the Tower of London alive that day.

The letter went on to suggest an arrangement whereby she and Hastings would together rule through the young king. 'My lords' said Richard 'you constitute a court of law here. In fact this is the highest court of law in the land. We have here a clear proof of treason to the State of England. I do not propose that we indict the queen for she is but a weak woman and is also mother to our present king, but you may all, my lords read what Lord Hastings has written. I propose that when you have read this letter, if you find him guilty, he should die this day!' One by one the lord of the Council read the letter and one by one they proclaimed Hastings guilty. He was taken out to the green and beheaded.

Richard charged his men to keep the other lords whom he had had arrested carefully, and with the dignity due to the Church and to the status of barons.

Then he closed the meeting. He had still to discuss the news of King Edward's false marriage more fully, but he could not face doing that until he had spoken with his wife and his mother. Sick at heart Richard went back to Baynard's Castle, his mother's home beside the river Thames.

Chapter 32.

At Baynard's Castle Again.

Richard entered his mother's house feeling downcast and in dread. As he went up the stairs to his mother's solar he had no idea of what awaited him. His heart was heavy for he was not a man to order a death penalty, and to see it executed, lightly and without careful thought. He had been shocked and horrified to find that the man whom his late brother had most loved and trusted as a friend could now turn traitor. That troubled and grieved him; to say nothing of his brother's marriage tangles.

A servant announced his presence and he entered his mother's chamber. A wonderful surprise greeted him! Sitting with lady Cecily his beloved mother was his even more beloved wife. 'Anne! My Anne!' he cried and crossed the room in two strides to sweep her into his arms. Then he remembered his manners 'My greetings to you my lady mother!' he called over Anne's shoulder. Lady Cecily was laughing at the two lovers locked in each others arms, yet still trying to include her in their happiness. 'Richard' said his mother, 'pray allow my lady your wife to be seated again. We both wish to speak to you!' Richard placed Anne on a bench seat and sat down beside her, taking her hand. 'How long have you been here, my dearest? Are you well after the journey?' he was full of questions. Anne was smiling at him her eyes bright as were his now that he had her beside him.

'I have not long arrived, my Richard. We made the journey quite easily, considering the great distance!' she told him, 'I left all in order at Middleham, the steward and Thomas, your secretary's young clerk, have their orders and before you ask me the children are all well!' she told him. Richard leaned back to look at her more clearly. 'You are no plumper my Anne!' he said 'No', she replied 'but I shall be soon – see how you mother is feeding me sugar cakes! I shall have to loosen my girdle if we stay here!' Lady Cecily clicked her tongue 'Now don't tell him such stories!' she exclaimed 'You have only eaten one! She is too thin. Diccon, what do you feed her on in Yorkshire that she is so slender? I thought they lived on cheese and baked custards in Wensley Dale!' Richard laughed and then he said that he would take Anne to Crosby's Place, their London home but his mother begged him that they should stay with her for a while 'I see little of you, Diccon, and rarely anything of your pretty Anne! We will make you both very comfortable here as you have been until now; there is no need to run away. I will arrange for the great bed to be moved into the chamber you are using. I am sure Anne would like to stay with me, would you not, Anne? Your husband is busy with matters of State and you and I will be company for each other while he is so taken up with the Court.' So it was arranged. Anne was happy to stay with her good-mother and she also expected more of Friar Luke's remedies to arrive there.

That night Anne and Richard lay together in the great old bed with the rich hangings that had been made for Richard's mother and father when they were about to be married. The same one in which they had passed their marriage night. The Thames ran close to their window so the sound of water could be clearly heard as they lay silent together arms entwined. They had not even undressed as yet and were simply resting. Richard was trying to forget the day's political matters which so disturbed him, and Anne was stretching her tired body after riding so long in the litter. Sensing that his thoughts were far away Anne laid her hand on his sleeve. Richard looked down and was shocked, for her hand looked like a flame. He blinked and looked again. Then he realized that she was so thin and her hand so fragile that the dull gold and dark crimson of his brocade doublet showed though her skin. Horrified he held her closely against him. 'Have you been careful to take the remedies that I have procured for you, dearest love? 'Yes my Richard, I have been most careful to do all that you have told me to do' she answered, 'and I have more remedies from Luke; he sent them to me as we came through the country and more are to come here. Why do you ask my love? I always do as you bid me!' 'And your cough?' he asked. Anne looked sad 'I still cough, my Richard, but I am well! I am so well now that you and I are together. I love you so much that I cannot eat when we are apart and that is why I get thin!'

Richard kissed her 'You are so precious to me, my Lady of Love!' He told her and his blue eyes were deep with desire, 'May I lie with you this night? We have been apart so long!' She crept closer into his side 'My Richard! I want you, too!' she murmured. Gently he unlaced her gown and she slipped out of her shift as he disrobed and then with great courtesy and delicacy he took his wife. She responded with her usual sweet passion and they moved together in tune with the wash of the tide on the Thames. That night they had both slept blissfully deep, for both had travelled in different ways, for many miles. They arose later than usual. Lady Cecily had forbidden anyone to awaken them for she knew well the sadness of being parted from a beloved spouse, and the joy of reunion.

Cecily had sat for a long time in her chamber the previous night thinking over the news that she had heard. She knew that her son, her only son now, was worried. She knew too that there was trouble brewing and that there had been ever since the splendid figure of her son Edward had left the stage. She wondered what the next dénouement would be.

Chapter 33.

What Marriage?

Next day, leaving Anne to rest in the great bed a little longer for he was concerned for her health after her long journey, Richard sought out his mother. Lady Cecily was busy with her household accounts and correspondence but she closed her ledgers and pushed them aside when her son entered her private room. This was a small chamber apart from her bedchamber and solar. Had it been a man's room it might have been called a study. It was here that Cecily read her letters and dealt with matters of her estate. Here she kept her religious books and it was where she retired when she required privacy. 'How do you this morning, my son?' 'I am well, mother, and so happy to be reunited with my wife!' 'That I am certain of Diccon but I see that you are troubled. What is it that causes you so much concern, my son?' Richard's mother was worried about him for the little upright lines between her son's brows were prominent and she guessed that he suffered from his spine as well as his thoughts.

'Mother will you tell me what you know of Edward's marriage to the lady Grey?' he asked. She was surprised 'Like you and the rest of the world I knew nothing of that! It was a shock to me as it was to all who knew him.' Richard was silent for a moment then he asked 'And did you hear rumours of a previous marriage? This is of great importance, mother.'

It was a few seconds before she answered for she had to think back over a long time. Then she said 'I did not hear of any marriage, my son, but I had expected to hear of one some long time before he married the lady Grey. I remember that Edward was much enamoured of the Lady Eleanor Butler. She was a great beauty who carried herself like a queen and who was highly born, a daughter of the Lord Talbot. She was the widow of the lord Butler. He was a Lancastrian, although her family were for the House of York. We all knew Edward was pursuing her, and knowing her for a pious and God-fearing lady we did not believe that she would allow that pursuit to prosper unless it was by marriage. But it seemed that nothing came of it, for although he granted her wealthy lands she never came to Court. Indeed, she retired to the country and, as I believe, to a nunnery. He had a mistress, he called her Lucy, a pretty little light of love, the first of many.' she looked sad 'I feel for Elizabeth Grey for she has not had so happy a marriage with my son Edward.' she said.

'She has had no marriage at all with Edward, mother!' Richard had blurted out the awful truth feeling safe with his mother. Lady Cecily looked aghast 'What do you mean, Richard?' Richard shrugged 'Just that, mother. It seems that Edward did marry the lady Eleanor. Robert Stillington married them and he came to me himself to tell me of this marriage. He has pointed out to me that Edward's sons are therefore base born for their parents never had a true marriage. What is worse, mother, is that this was why Edward would show no mercy to my brother of Clarence. George was imprisoned in the Tower of London after one of hiss foolish escapades and at the same time Father Stillington was also there. He told him of Ned's marriage to the Lady Eleanor after George had plied him with drink.' Lady Cecily was silent for a moment then she asked 'Are you certain of this, Diccon? Did Stillington have any writings to confirm these assertions?' 'He has nothing to show but he has offered to affirm all this in a court of law' Richard replied. 'Mother, he says that this previous marriage means that the marriage to the lady Grey was bigamous and that their children are all base born and because of this young Edward cannot be crowned!' 'I think he is right. And I fear the consequences! The Queen's family are very powerful.' lady Cecily said, and she sounded worried.

Richard was pacing the room. He stopped to gaze out of the window, looking at the Thames as it rolled past his mother's walls. 'What will happen mother?' he asked. 'I don't know, my dear,' he mother said 'but I can see that if young Edward is not legitimate he cannot be king; and as Clarence was declared a traitor his son cannot inherit the throne. That leaves just one person as the next heir.' She spoke very softly as if she were afraid of spies overhearing her. 'Who is that, mother?' asked Richard. Cecily clicked her tongue at him, 'Do you really not know my lad? It's you, you silly fellow! Who else can it be?' her son looked at her in total disbelief. 'Me? It cannot be me. I have to guard the north of England mother. I cannot be a king!' 'Well whether you like it or not you are the next heir.' she said, rather crossly. Richard came back to stand beside her chair. 'Can you not think of someone else? I have no wish to sit in my brother's chair!' He sounded so childlike that Cecily lost patience 'Well then just get a new chair built, one that you do like, and sit in that. For you will be the king. You have to be, for there is no other.' Richard put his head in his hands. This news was not to his liking. And he realized now that his mother was right. 'I will go and find Anne,' he said 'Mother. I do love you and I am sorry if I have made you angry with me!' 'I am not angry with you, Richard! Now then! Just remember that you are a Plantagenet and that your own father had a better right to the throne than poor mad Henry did!' she kissed him and he knelt for her blessing. Then he kissed her cheek, and left her.

Chapter 34.

Buckingham and Richard Confer.

Richard sent word to the duke of Buckingham requesting him to visit Barnard's Castle. The Duke arrived in a short time and Richard explained that his brother's infatuation with lady Eleanor had been well known to his mother and to many others at court and that while still married to her he had married lady Grey, so that his marriage to the queen was bigamous and their children bastards.

'We must discuss this in Parliament.' said Buckingham, 'for this matter is of concern to all England. The members must know of it!'

Parliament met and Richard attended as did Bishop Stillington and the other nobles of the land. There were several matters to be discussed but first of all Buckingham told the assembly that young Edward's coronation could not now happen as had been arranged. He told them of Bishop Stillington's revelation and suggested that all the most venerable and learned Church Fathers should meet to discuss whether or not the late king's marriage to the lady Elizabeth Grey was a legal marriage in the sight of God and Holy Church and if it was not to decide whether their son may or may not be crowned. This news was of utmost importance and the members agreed that the Church fathers should be consulted.

The assembly then broke up and lords and commons went their ways, all discussing how to proceed and wondering how the Church Fathers would decide. Richard went home to Barnard's Castle. He could not find either Anne or his mother.

Going to his mother private room he tapped on the door. 'If that is you, my son, you may enter' said his mother. Richard pushed the door open and went in. Lady Cecily was again working on her books. She laid down her quill and half-turned in her chair to face him, 'Welcome, King Richard!' she said 'Oh, mother, do not call me that!' her son cried and his face was ashen 'There must be someone else who will be a suitable king. I am just a soldier - simply a soldier of fortune if truth be told for all that I have I have earned from my brother Edward by my sword!'

'You have also proved yourself a just ruler and a good law giver' said his mother. Richard sat down on a stool at the other side of her desk. 'Mother, I have no desire to be a king.' He said 'I am happy to guard the northern borders and will go on doing so but not as king!' he protested. 'Will you then allow the Widow Grey and her rapacious family to rule this land, to its destruction?' she asked. Richard groaned. 'No that is not what I want! Is there no one else with a better claim than I have?' 'No, Diccon, there is not since we now know that young Edward is not eligible.' said his mother. Richard persisted 'But we do not know that yet, mother!' Cecily looked at him her face grave 'We will soon see' she said 'Go now and comfort Anne she is in her bed tired out from the journey. And I hope she is asleep!' She turned away and picked up her quill. Richard knew that his mother had dismissed him. Dutifully he went to the chamber he shared with his wife.

He found his beloved Anne there. She was asleep in their great bed and he would not wake her. He undressed very quietly and slid naked into the space beside her. In her sleep she turned to him smiling and murmuring his name. He felt better. Anne loved him and he could do anything so long as Anne still loved him. Although it was broad day he also slept,

Richard had a visitor just after he had broken his fast next day. 'My lord, the lord duke of Buckingham seeks an audience with you' his mother's steward said sounding rather more pompous than usual 'Well, let him come in man, let him come in!' said Richard. And Buckingham walked into the room swept off his rather gorgeous hat and said 'Good morrow, my Liege' 'What was that?' Richard spluttered into his small ale 'What did you say?' Buckingham laughed 'I said 'Good Morrow, my Liege'' he repeated. Richard looked aghast. 'What game is this, my lord?' he demanded. 'It is no game.' Buckingham told him, 'Richard of Gloucester I am come to offer you the crown of England which is yours by right of inheritance.' Richard had never felt so terrified in his life. Not since he stood at the market cross at Ludlow!

'Come and sit down Buckingham and please, just tell me what is happening!.' he said. Buckingham came to join Richard at the table and sat opposite him.

'Well to start at the beginning' he explained 'all the Fathers of the Church put their heads together in a secret conference last night. They questioned Bishop Stillington and they believe his story. Someone was sent to the queen to ask her if she knew anything of this. She refused to see the man that they sent or to discuss this mater with anyone at all.

So bearing all this in mind and given the secret nature of her presumed and clearly clandestine marriage to our late king and knowing his propensity for pursuit of any woman at any price, they and Parliament have commissioned me to ask you to accept the crown. There is of course Clarence's lad but his father was declared a traitor so that his lands are forfeit; and he is a minor anyway. So as you are next in line Richard of Gloucester, will you accept the crown of England?'

Richard sat quite still with his chin propped on his hands and his elbows on the table. 'I need time to think' he said. 'Of course' said Buckingham, 'that is understandable. But please do not make your thinking last too long a time for the whole country is waiting leaderless at this moment. Who knows what catastrophe may occur while you ponder!' Richard shook his head, trying to think clearly. 'How long a time have I got?' he asked 'Great Heavens, Richard! I am asking you to be king not telling you that you are going to the gallows!' Buckingham was laughing now. 'You have some hours,' he told Richard, 'I shall escort you to Westminster Hall after dinner.' 'So it is all planned?' Richard asked 'Yes it is all planned.' Buckingham grinned. Then he said 'You can do this Gloucester! You are a good administrator and a good leader of men.' 'But I am not like my brother the late king.' said Richard of Gloucester 'No that is true. You are not like king Edward your brother and that is just as well! You are a man who loves his wife and who does his best to keep the law and the Peace. And you are as good a warrior as your brother ever was. You have proved that over and again. You do not chase women or drink too heavily and waste time on foolish things. You will be good for England because you love your country and are just and fair minded and have studied the law! Come, now, Gloucester! Believe me! You know the law better than Edward did and you will make a good king. I wish I could say the same for myself.' There was just a hint of bitterness in his tone. Richard recalled with just the hint of a shiver that Buckingham had royal ancestors too; the same ancestors as he had himself.

'Very well, I will come,' he said, 'but first I must inform my lady wife and the lady Cecily my mother. And I suppose I must change my shirt.' Buckingham roared with laughter and slapped Richard on the back. 'You will make a wonderful king' he said 'especially if you change your shirt!'

Chapter 35.

Richard is offered the Crown.

With great promptitude Buckingham appeared immediately after dinner, which Richard had not been able to eat at all. Buckingham was accompanied by other lords and great Worthies of the City of London who all begged Richard to accept the Crown of England. Buckingham also announced his intention to convey the Duke of Gloucester to Westminster Hall to meet with the other members of the Lords and Commons and to request Richard to accept the Crown of England in a proper and formal manner and in public.

By now Richard had had time to tell Anne that she was about to become the queen of England and he had also spoken with his mother. Having prepared both ladies for this new arrangement he had agreed to accept the honour bestowed upon him. He went with Anne to his mother's little chapel where they both prayed. Richard prayed that he would be a good king and that he would always have courage to stand against evil doers and to uphold the laws of England. Anne prayed for her husband and for the strength to support him with her love. Then they rejoined the gathering who awaited them in the great room of Baynard's Castle

Richard squared his shoulders and went with Buckingham in a barge to Westminster. As they floated along on the Thames Richard was very quiet for h was thinking hard. At last he told Buckingham his intentions for the sons of Edward the Fourth.

'I intend to place my brother's sons at Sheriff Hutton with my own children and George's lad.' He said 'For if they remain here in the City there will undoubtedly be an attempt on someone's part to make young Edward king and to rule in his name. The place swarms with the queen's relatives and friends and those whom she and her affinity have bought. We cannot have more unrest. Remember poor king Henry and the troubles that his madness caused!'

'I agree with you. We must avoid disruption and bloodshed' said Buckingham 'I will see that they are safely conveyed from the Royal Apartments in the Tower to your castle at Sheriff Hutton' Richard nodded 'Please do so.' he said 'And Buckingham, please see that they are taken there by someone they trust and like. Is King Edward's steward still in London? He and his wife would be a most excellent choice because the two lads know them well. I will ensure that they are provided for as well as my own children, for my brother loved them, and I am sworn in loyalty to him to care for them! And that man of Edward's will be in need of a place, for I will have my own choice of servants about me.' Buckingham promised to see the two boys safely installed with Richard's children and his other wards and also to search out the steward.

By this time they had arrived at Westminster. There were guardsmen waiting to escort them to the Hall. Inside the Hall, Richard walked up the length of the long building and then took his on the marble 'King's Bench' used only by the king when he sat in judgement. He was now, whether he liked it or not, king of England.

The Duke of Buckingham had persuaded Richard to accept the crown of England and had conducted Richard of Gloucester into Westminster Hall where Richard sat on the marble seat, 'The King's Bench' that was used only by the monarch sitting in judgement. He was formally asked to accept the crown. He acquiesced but spoke humbly of his duty to Parliament and to the people of the realm.

155

Richard had already sent to York to request some of his guardsmen to travel to London from Yorkshire because he believed that there may be a rising of the queen's friends who would target both the duke of Buckingham and himself. These men arrived as soon as they could march south and Richard felt all the safer for their presence. There had been some disturbances in the some of the streets of London when it became known that Lord Hastings had been executed. He had been a friend of the late king and was popular for that reason Edward having been much admired by the common people as well as the gentry. Hastings had been wealthy and open handed with his gold so that he had gained followers in that way too. Richard called out the guards together with his Yorkshire men and the disturbances were quieted.

Meanwhile young Edward and Richard, the sons of King Edward the fourth, were taken privately to live with their various cousins at Sheriff Hutton castle. Edward was now known as 'the lord Bastard' and he was neither well nor happy. It had been explained to him that his parents' marriage was not valid and he obviously had to accept this as the reason why he was not crowned as he had expected. He had not been a sturdy lad although an intelligent and well educated one. His general health was not good and he had trouble with his cheek bone which hurt as if a tooth was not coming through properly.

His uncle Richard and his aunt Anne hoped that the good air of Yorkshire and the company of his sibling and his cousins would help his well being. Careful accounts were made of expenditure at the castle and good food was high on the list. In fact the castle had become something like a school for aristocratic youngsters.

The whereabouts of the two sons of King Edward the fourth was not made public for the precise reasons that Richard had

had them placed at Sheriff Hutton. Sadly, the fact that the boys were no longer seen in London gave rise to rumours that they had been murdered and that this crime had possibly been committed by their uncle Richard or at his instigation.

Chapter 36.

King Richard and Queen Anne

On the sixth day of July in the year of Our Lord 1483, Richard Plantagenet and Anne Neville processed to Westminster Abbey and were crowned king and Queen in the most splendid coronation that had ever been seen. After this there was held an equally splendid and lavish feast at which practically the whole nobility of England were present; the only absentees being those too old or infirm or too young to attend. During the feast the King's Champion ride into the hall on a white charger and in white armour and threw down his gauntlet, challenging anyone who did not agree that Richard was the rightful king.
The whole company shouted 'King Richard' then the Champion drank the king's health threw down the rest of his wine and then rode of with the costly bejewelled goblet as his fee.
At that time a document was prepared in which was an explanation of what had occurred in the royal family and why Richard was the next in line to the throne. A priest also preached a sermon at Paul's Cross, explaining what had occurred to change the line of accession. There were of course those who did not like the new arrangements. And Queen Elizabeth and her extended family had lost much power.
As soon as he possibly could Richard found time to talk to his wife at greater length than there had been time for previously. As at last they laid in their great bed that night both weary from the day's events he said 'My Dearest Lady of Love, this is an honour that I had never expected and a task which I cannot lightly perform. My Anne! I shall need your love and support

even more now!' she answered him at once 'It is of course going to be a great task, my Richard, but I know that you will perform it honourably and well. And of course you have my support, such as it is, for you know how much I love you!' Richard took her into his warm and loving embrace and said 'My Lady of Love! I will do my best to be a good king and to remain a loving husband and father. With you beside me I feel stronger; you, my Love, will be an ornament to the crown! For you are so sweet and gentle a lady that I do not doubt that the people will love you as I do.' Anne smiled at him. 'Dearest husband,' she replied 'I am sure that when they know you for the just and merciful man that you are they will bless God for sending them Richard for their king!' and she kissed him sweetly.

At the dizzy height of kingship they found it harder to find moments alone. They could no longer slip away unnoticed to their great bed whenever they chose. And after the Coronation celebrations it became necessary for them to go on a series if progresses so that the people of England could see and meet with their king and queen. Privacy was harder to find yet they managed somehow to find moments alone.

  In Court circles it soon became known that unlike most royal couples King Richard and his Queen always shared a bed. 'I cannot bear to be separated from you, my Anne!' said Richard as they entered the bed chamber prepared for them on the first night of their first progress together. Anne had stayed in London for a while and had joined him at Warwick. 'It seems we are considered to be a strange king and queen because we always sleep together!' he told her. Anne laughed 'I am certain that we are, my Richard, for we were married for love and not for political gain or as some national necessity.' Richard mused 'It is true.' he said 'I was a third son and so was never intended to be a king. And neither did I wish to be one and thus I was able to declare my love for you and choose you for my wife. And I thank God for that!' His only great concern was that Anne's cough was getting worse and she could no longer hide from him that she bled when she coughed. No remedy could be found that worked the miracle that he prayed for so constantly.

Wherever the progresses took him Richard was welcomed by the common people as well as by the mayors and local noblemen for his reputation for fairness and justice went before him. He spent long hours listening to poor men and poor women telling him of their troubles. He would always help them and if they were being oppressed by anyone no matter how great a lord their oppressor might be, they had redress from King Richard.

One day as he was riding beside her litter on yet another progress Anne asked 'Do you feel more comfortable as king now, my Richard?' Richard thought for a moment the lines between his brows furrowing. 'I cannot say that I enjoy kingship for itself,' he said as he thought carefully 'but I enjoy finding out about the people and I am glad to be able to put right a few matters which should have been righted before this'. Anne asked him what he meant. 'Well, my Anne, I am determined that all law must be conducted in the English language for most people now do not understand the debased Norman French or the dog Latin used by lawyers and even by Parliament in their Acts. We speak all English in these days, so why is the law written in a foreign tongue which is understood by few? And why use it in the law courts? The people cannot know if justice is being done.'

He jogged along in silence for a while and then he said 'Here is another matter that has come to my notice. There came a woman begging me for justice for her husband. It seems that he had been imprisoned for theft but his trial had not taken place in a whole year. She could prove that her man was not the thief and she had no-one to support her and her children while he rotted in a prison. That is not justice my Anne! And I shall find a way to ensure that such things do not happen.'

After a little while he suddenly said 'I have it! That man was in prison accused of stealing four pence. Now if he were to be allowed to leave prison on the understanding that he would pay four pence if he was found guilty at trial and that someone would pay the four pence on his behalf if he did not attend his trial then he could go home and support his family for the time before the trial took place. That would be fair would it not?'

Anne agreed that the idea was a good one and just.

Richard had invented the system of bail.

As the first part of their progresses Richard visited many of his cities granting Charters to some, including to the City of Gloucester which was his name place and seeing that justice was done there as in every place that he visited.. Then he took the road to Tewkesbury where he had helped bring his older brother to the throne. He stopped there and went into the Abbey to pray for those who died on that day of battle. And he also prayed for his brother George and his sister in law Isabel interred there. He remembered with gratitude the late prince Edward, whose death in battle had allowed him to wed his beloved lady Anne,

Then he progressed on his way through the Midlands.

 At every place where he and his entourage stopped he sent the local nobles away after making them promise to uphold the law and treat the people who lived and worked on their estates with fairness. Men spoke of him as a good lord.

Chapter 37.

York!

One of the places that Richard and Anne most wished to visit was the city of York. They arrived there in September when the glorious stone of the town and the Minster glowed in gentle sunlight. The welcome that they received was almost overwhelming! The noise of bells and trumpets as they rode through the gates was deafening and there were garlands and beautiful cloths hanging everywhere and draped at every window. Cheering people in coloured clothing flocked around them in hundreds.

Richard did not travel with any guards so that the common people could truly see him and approach him to ask him for his help if they wished to do so.

Richard was very popular in the city of York, as was Anne, because they had lived nearby for so long and had often been visitors there. At the Minster they gave thanks for their elevation to the throne which they both felt had come as an unexpected honour. They were able to attend the Guild of Corpus Christi to which they both belonged and renewed acquaintance with the other Guild members

To their great joy their young son Ned came to be with his parents. He had grown taller but was not as robust as his father would have liked and had had to travel in a chariot. 'Never fear, Anne, my love! He will grow stronger!' Richard told his wife. In a moment of great splendour and solemnity Ned was dubbed a knight (to his great joy) and then installed as Prince of Wales. The King and Queen and the Prince all wore their crowns and their most regal garments which had been sent from the Royal Wardrobe in London for the occasion. Afterwards they were treated to a huge and splendid feast and banquet, given by the city worthies. (This was actually rather boring for Ned although he behaved perfectly!)

Richard in return for so splendid a welcome reduced the taxes payable by the City of York by half to the great joy of the burgesses and people.

Richard was offered gold cups full of coins wherever he went but he always refused them and instead asked what he could do the help the local people. The opinion of all was that he was a good and just Prince and sent by God for their comfort and wellbeing. People were very happy to have a king who actually cared for them and who understood their lives and their difficulties and really tried to make their lives a little better.

Concerned about the floods that happened so often in Somerset where the rivers overflowed the arable and pasture land Richard asked Anne 'What can we do to help these poor souls. They work so hard only to see their lands washed clean of crops and grazing!' Having thought a little his wife reminded him of the men of the Low Countries, beyond the sea, 'Why, yes!' he cried. 'They know much about draining land!' He found men from the Low Countries who understood such matters and set them to work to improve the situation.

The new king also realized that there were men who took for themselves names and blazons of arms to which they had no right therefore he set up the College of Heralds to look into who was a rightfully am armiger and to draw up blazons of arms for those who had been granted them. This was to stop unlawful use of other men's signets this was important at a time when few ordinary folk could write and seals were the substitute for a signature.

Anne was so proud of her husband. Not only was he young and handsome but he was kind and caring. This was not only to their family and affinity but to all his subjects. She put her hand gently on his and said 'My Richard! I am very glad that you are king of England. This is not because of the glory of wearing a crown or because people bow to us. I am happy that you are doing so many things that will help the people. You are especially helping the poor and those who are in trouble. This was what you did for the people in Yorkshire and your other lands and I am so proud of you!' Richard looked down at her hand and saw how thin it was 'My beloved Anne!' he said 'It is my work as a king to care for my people and to see that justice is done and the law maintained. I must also take care of the land where they live and work. That is the promise that I made when I was crowned.'

Chapter 38.

September 1483. Rebellion!

Hardly had the celebrations for Ned's installation been completed than Richard received almost unbelievable news.

On the eighth day October in the year of our Lord 1483 and only three months after Richard's coronation a messenger came hot foot from the south with a letter from London. A rebellion had broken out in the southern counties. Stirred up by the Woodville faction the intention was to find the two sons of Edward the Fourth and to place Edward the older of the two on the throne. What was incomprehensible to Richard was that the man he had thought was his friend had joined the rebels. The Duke of Buckingham had joined forces with the Woodvilles. He had always maintained that he disliked the whole family. Now he was making common cause with them.

Richard knew that he must act at once to stamp out this rebellion. Anne was shocked. 'Harry of Buckingham was your friend!' she exclaimed 'It was he who offered you the crown! He was insistent that you become king. Why has he suddenly changed?' Her husband's brows furrowed as he said 'I do not know his motives. He has a claim to the throne through his descent from the same ancestors as mine and it may be that he thinks he would make a better king than do I!' He was silent for a long moment and then he said 'You will recall that I arrested Bishop Morton for his treasonable actions. Buckingham was very anxious to have custody of Bishop Morton and under his watch the bishop was allowed more freedom to have visitors that I would have liked. And I have information that the Lady Elizabeth Grey's man visited him. I

165

wonder if there was always a deeper plot that Buckingham planned. A plot planned so deep that I could never have guessed of it!'

Then it became known that the Duke of Buckingham had proclaimed that the sons of the late King had been murdered. He did not actually accuse King Richard of this crime but it was natural that many people assumed that that was what he meant. It was suggested that the two boys had been killed in the Tower of London when they were lodged in the royal Apartments in readiness for the coronation of young Edward, before the revelation of their parents' invalid marriage.

Richard knew where the boys were and that they were safe. He also knew that Edward was not a very sturdy lad and suffered with his jaw. This was thought to be a result of some teeth being slow in coming, but no-one had found a remedy for his discomfort. Anne urged her husband to announce the whereabouts of the lads.

She begged in vain. Richard would not stoop to refute a crime that he had not committed. Nor would he bring the boys to public view. Richard had good intelligence of what was happening in the kingdom and that there were those who disputed his rights. But he was appalled to find how many of the nobility and gentry had joined in this rebellion. Richard also knew that Buckingham had lingered in London after the he and Anne had set out on their first progress. Buckingham could have made all kinds of plots!

Now it became known that Buckingham had been in contact with Elizabeth, lately Queen, and with Lady Margaret Beaufort and her son Henry Tudor. The depth of his treachery was a sad blow to the King.

Taking a sad leave of his wife Richard rode swiftly south. By the twelfth day of October he had reached Lincoln and from there he wrote to Lord Chancellor Russell to request that the Great Seal be brought to. Without the Seal no documents were legal so that Richard wanted it in his own keeping. He also asked Lord Russell to come himself and wrote of his determination to quell the rebellion. This he did as quickly as he could and he was aided in this by the bad weather and the disloyalty of Buckingham's own retainers. They had destroyed the bridges that Buckingham needed to cross in order to join up the two separate arms of the rebellion.

Henry Tudor had put to sea at Buckingham's request but the atrocious weather made it impossible for him to land. Meanwhile the duke of Buckingham had raised his own standard in Exeter. When Henry Tudor did not arrive with his followers Buckingham made for Salisbury, which town King Richard had already reached. There on the first day of November the rebel duke was arrested by the King's men and the next day he was executed. The whole rebellion then collapsed.

Richard was appalled that one who had appeared to have been his friend and whom he had trusted so much, had turned against him. 'I realize now that Buckingham's reason for befriending me was entirely selfish' he told Anne, 'I gave him lands and wealth and high office and he used that wealth and that power for his own ends' Anne nodded, 'Yes, my Richard, his intention must have been to get the throne for himself although the rebellion supposed to be in the name of Henry Tudor'. Richard who had been loyal all his life to his family and friends alike, found this a hard lesson to learn. 'I will not make one man so powerful again' he told his wife. The lack of loyalty in the man he had so much trusted was a bitter blow.

To add to his concerns he could see his beloved Anne becoming more and more pale and wan. He tried hard to hide his worries from her because he wanted her to be happy and at peace so that her health might improve. His own feelings were far from peaceful. Now that so many erstwhile 'friends' had shown their true colours and so many of them had fled across the sea who was he to trust? Richard began to place his northern friends in places of trust and influence. He had learned that they were staunch friends and so it was natural that he turned to them when others who were traitors had fled abroad,

Richard and Anne celebrated the first Christmas of their reign with many of Richard's northern friends now about him. These were people whom he and Anne knew well and whom they knew they could trust. Richard was also in communication with his late brother's widow and this eased some of the tensions that he felt around him. She had agreed that her daughters might now come to Court.

Anne greeted her nieces politely and as warmly as she could and was kind to them. She made gifts of dresses and fine fabrics to these girls who had been treated as princesses. They were the daughters of a king and deserved to be well dressed and well placed at Court.

At about this time Richard arranged a marriage for Katherine his natural daughter. She was to marry William Herbert the Earl of Huntingdon. Anne was concerned for Katherine's happiness. 'Are you sure that your daughter will be happy, my Richard?' she asked. 'Why do you ask me that, Sweetheart?' he said 'Poor Katherine is not to be married for love as we were!' Anne replied, but Richard explained 'She has met him and she likes him. I have settled a large dower on her so she will want for nothing. He is a good man and has promised to care for her. She may not be as lucky as we were my Anne, and marry for love alone, but I will watch over her. Never fear!'

168

Anne ensured that the young countess-to-be had all that she needed as regards a wardrobe befitting a king's daughter and that she understood what the physical part of marriage entailed. She had loved Richard's natural children as if they were her own. 'I am glad that she is to be settled in life' said Katherine's stepmother 'I hope that William will be as gentle with her on her wedding night as you were with me!' Richard embraced her noting sadly how slender she had become 'Never fear, my Anne,' he said 'all will be well. I have told him that she is dear to me and must be treasured and treated with kindness and gentleness!'

Chapter 39.

The Year of Our Lord 1484

In January of the Year of Our Lord 1484 Richard called a
Parliament. All went well
and the document named 'Titulus Regius' was proclaimed.
This set out King Richard's clear right to the throne of
England.
The Lady Elizabeth who had once been queen of England was
welcomed back to Court on the first day of March and Anne
greeted her and made her welcome.
Queen Anne was especially friendly with Elizabeth's eldest
daughter who was also named Elizabeth. These two young
women found that they had shared tastes in dresses and
jewellery and in books and music. They spent much time in
each other's company and as the King liked to be with his wife
whenever possible the young Elizabeth grew to know him too.
She began to comprehend how hard he had worked for her late
father King Edward and to understand his quiet sense of
humour and gentle fun. She also began to appreciate why her
Aunt Anne loved him so much and she saw how much that
love was returned. Elizabeth came to realize how hard a king
had to work and she wondered how her sweet aunt Anne
managed when her husband was so very busy, but she knew
how much Anne with her love, supported King Richard in his
work.
Richard was often away from Court for there were problems on
the borders with Scotland and he went to oversee the army the
Brave young Earl of Lincoln in charge, and Richard was

pleased with what he was doing. Then Richard had to meet with an embassy from France.

It was difficult for Richard to organize his foreign policy. He told Anne 'My brother the king made peace with France, but he had previously made a treaty with Burgundy. The duke of Burgundy had taken us in, Edward and me, when Edward lost his throne for a little while' 'Do you mean when my father and George of Clarence rebelled against King Edward and reinstalled poor Henry?' Anne asked. Richard was a little embarrassed, 'Yes' he said 'We stayed in Burgundy then. They were kind to us and so I feel that we owe them our friendship.' Anne nodded, 'I see that this is the case' she said 'What will you do, my Richard?' He was puzzled. 'I do not quite know what I should do. I believe sometimes one should wait upon events.' he replied. Anne took his hand. 'I am sure there are many things in England that need your attention' she said 'you can concern your self with the French later on!' Richard knew that he would have to be wary of the Scots as well as the French and the home-grown rebels but he did not wish to alarm his wife. She was less and less healthy and he seemed unable to find a physician who could help her.

Richard dropped a kiss on to the top of her head 'Wise Lady of Love!' he said 'Let us sleep on this!' and he led her to their great bed.

In spring it was time to go on progress once again. They set off with Anne riding in her letter and Richard riding beside her on his favourite White Surrey. Richard had reasons for going north. He wished to meet with his forces to meet him at Newcastle for he had thought to settle some outstanding military business with the Scots. Then he and Anne rode through as many towns as they could, all the while Richard was busy attending to the concerns of the people. They reached

171

Nottingham at the beginning of March and were well received and lodged in the castle. Many great events were planned and the king and queen looked forward to some entertainment, before Richard's serious business began. They were happy together and hopeful.

The world was plunged into sadness and darkness for Richard and Anne when a messenger arrived.

He was tired and covered in mud from the roads and he brought the worst tidings that

Richard and Anne could ever hear.

Their son Edward was dead.

He had succumbed to a cough similar to that from which his mother suffered. Being so young and not robust to start with, the disease had worked its terrible wrath upon him in a very short time.

The poor bereaved parents were distraught. An onlooker described them as being like mad people in their grief.

Anne tried to comfort Richard and Richard tried to comfort Anne but there was no comfort to be had. They had only ever had one child. Anne had never again conceived in spite of her pilgrimages and prayers.

Not knowing what else to do Anne sent for Friar Luke. He came as fast as the horse that he had could go and the road that they travelled on would allow.

Luke went at once to the king and spoke gently to Richard. He told him that such a young soul as his son's would not suffer purgatory. He described how holy angels would have conducted the boy's soul to Heaven there to be received by his Saviour and by the Father and the Holy Ghost..

Luke told Anne the same, but she blamed herself for not giving her beloved Richard more than one child. She was so frail herself and so wracked with grief, that even Luke's words hardly penetrated the fog of sorrow that surrounded her.

Luke prayed with the bereaved parents and did his best to restore them to some semblance of sanity. But for all his help Anne's cough worsened and Richard's mood became more sombre. From then onwards Richard called Nottingham 'My Castle of Care'. And though he stayed there, putting off all other journeys, he said he would not willingly visit there again.

In the little village church at Sheriff Hutton the small body of Anne's and Richard's only child, who was also their only hope, was laid to rest and a tombstone was erected over his grave. This was intended to be a temporary resting place for the young prince. His father had already instituted a college of one hundred priests at York Minster and an oratory was planned where Masses and prayers were to be said for the souls of those whom Richard loved. This was to be in perpetuity. Building had already begun on the place where Richard intended that he and Anne and their son would eventually be laid to rest.

Luke rode back to Leicester and to his Friary and he was heavy hearted for he could not but think that his Master Richard's lovely lady Queen Anne would surely follow her son to the grave before very much time had passed. He was sad for his Master Richard who carried so many cares. He knew him for a good man and a kindly one and Luke was distressed to hear scandalous stories spread about him. He felt certain that it would not be long before he was again called upon to comfort this quiet but often gently humorous man whose sense of justice he so much admired.

To find some comfort for her maternal longings Anne took under her wing the young son of Isabel her late sister. The poor boy had neither father nor mother and was glad of the kindness from his sweet aunt Anne. He was some small comfort to her since her loss

Richard worked hard for his country making good laws and trying to forge good relationships with other countries. Helped by his chosen men he did his best to rule with justice. He was also merciful to those whom he knew had been traitors. A very few executions had taken places after Buckingham's rebellion had been suppressed. Richard returned their lands to many of the wives and children of those who had rebelled against him. Their children were provided for, the boys being placed as Richard himself had been, in the households of gentlemen so that they might learn to be courteous and to follow knightly practice. The daughters were found good husbands of suitable rank. Indeed Anne often wondered if her husband was perhaps too gentle with his enemies!

Richard was busy with State documents one day when Anne came to confer with him on a matter of some visitors to their Court. 'What are you doing, my Richard?' she questioned 'I am reviewing the ships that are at our disposal, my Lady of Love' he told her 'Pirates are troubling my merchants' shipping. This land of ours relies on trade abroad, so I must find a way to stop this piracy. It is hard, for there are also English pirates which makes it more difficult to deal with those from other lands. The kings of Spain and France, and any other country, can point the finger at us and refuse to deal with their own miscreants. It is a puzzle that I must solve. Our merchants and their goods must be safe'. 'I am sure that you will find a way!' said Anne. Richard straightened up. And rubbed the middle of his back, which was sore from poring over the table. 'Dearest Anne!' he said 'I wish I could! I wish it were easier to deal with this and so many other problems. But I am at heart a simple soldier. I will just have to do the best I can!' and he kissed her. 'Go and rest, my love.' He said. But she wanted to stay with him for a little longer. So he sat with her, talking of old times and any happy things that he could think of for he saw that she was not only ill but also frightened.

All the while as the year went on Anne became less and less well. 'My dearest Anne, are you taking your medicines?' Richard asked her anxiously. 'Yes, my Richard. I always do what you ask of me!' she said. He embraced her very gently not to cause her to cough more 'I care for you so much, my Lady of Love!' he said 'And I so wish that we might find a cure for what ever it is that makes you so frail!' Anne smiled at him and laid her head on his chest so that she could hear his heart beating. She loved this sign of his life.

At Easter time there were celebrations at court and Anne tried hard to appear well. But Richard could see that she was failing fast. He still hoped that he might find a physician who could help her to recover her health. No one could. Everyone could see that the queen was going to die, and soon.

The year dragged on with Richard working hard to keep in tact that which his brother Edward had put into place while also ensuring that the commoners of his Realm were treated justly and fairly. Justice was his watch-word as much as loyalty and he left no stone unturned to ensure that justice was done. His work as king, over which he took minute care, made it ever more difficult to spend as much time as he would have wished with Anne. But they still shared a bed every night unless he was travelling away from Court. Their love was still strong but he now he no longer asked her for his conjugal rights for he knew how frail she had become. He contented himself with kissing her gently and saying a tender 'Good night, my Lady of Love'. Then Anne would curl up against his side and sleep.

Richard found sleep harder to capture as he held his beautiful, fragile and beloved wife in his arms.

Christmas came again at last and Anne made every attempt to celebrate with bright new clothes which the young lady Elizabeth had helped her to choose. Richard had prepared for a Yuletide with feasts and mummers, jugglers and dances and he hoped that some happiness might be found. And still he sought to find a doctor of medicine clever enough to save the life of the woman he loved.

There were singers and tumblers and much feasting and dancing. Many years later a very old lady would tell her great grandchildren of how handsome a man King Richard had been, even more handsome than his brother the splendid King Edward!

While she enjoyed the merry making Anne found it all very tiring. Her health was declining rapidly and she felt herself weakening daily. During that year's Christmas festivities it happened that Anne and her niece Elizabeth both wore gowns of the same colour and style for a feast 'Elizabeth and I bought too much of this beautiful stuff and we did not wish to waste any of it,' Anne told her husband 'so we have had gowns made to match,' she laughed 'people will not know which of us is which!'

'I will know, my Anne!' said Richard 'Do not imagine that you can fool me for you will not escape!' and he caught her around the waist and kissed her very thoroughly. 'There!' he said 'I have sealed you for myself, my lady of Love, and I will always see where you are!'

After the feast was over there was dancing and Richard danced with his wife first and then with his niece. He danced gracefully and people enjoyed watching the family of York disporting itself.

But later an ugly rumour grew from this innocent dance and the matching dresses.

Chapter 40.

Death of a Queen. 1485.

Eventually, early in the New Year Anne had to take to her bed.
Richard would to her when he had dealt with his day's work
and would hold her hand and talk to her of his love and
concern. She was often too weak and too tired from her fits of
coughing to answer him.
At last, in February of the year of Our Lord 1485, the queen's
physicians came to speak with the king. Richard received them
in some perplexity for he had taken such care to have his
beloved wife treated by the best doctors and physicians that
could be found.
Now they told him that he could no longer share his wife's bed
or even see her to speak with her.
Richard was horrified. 'You speak of my beloved wife!' he
said 'Why may I not see her? If she is sick she will need me. If
she is dying she will need my presence even more. I must go to
her! I will go to her, now and at once!' 'You must not do so,
your Grace' said the chief physician 'her Grace the queen is
too sick and her sickness is contagious. You are the King and
we must preserve your health' He looked very grave but
Richard tried again to persuade the doctors to let him see his
wife. 'Your Grace, we have moved her Grace to another
bedchamber. And we must have yours aired and cleansed, your
Grace, in case you take the contagion.'
Richard was in hell. His beloved Anne was barred from him
and he could not even see her from the doorway of the
bedchamber that they had so recently shared. Sadly he walked
away. Then he turned back to the physicians 'Have you told the

queen that we may not see each other?' asked 'And if you have
done so, did she have any message to my comfort?' he asked
them. One of them bowed low and said 'Your Grace, the queen
did speak of one named Friar. Luke. He is one, she said, who
will be of help to you' he bowed again and the physicians left
Richard alone in his grief and bewilderment.

'What does a man do', thought King Richard, 'when he is told
that his beloved wife is about to die and he may not bid her
farewell!' He twisted her little diamond ring on his smallest
finger and walked about the room aimlessly. Then he pulled
himself together and called Master Kendall to him. 'Kendall,
my friend,' he said 'I wish you to ride to Leicester and bring
Friar Luke to me. Tell him that my Lady Anne is about to die
and that I am refused permission to be with her. He must come
to me at once for I am in sore need of his help' 'Aye, that I will
your Grace' said Kendall, 'and I will bring him as soon as we
may get back to you. Two days, your Grace, is all it should
take' and he bowed and left.

Kendall went at once on the best horse he could find and rode
swiftly by the quickest route for Leicester.

Some of the lords of the Council waited upon their King. They
all looked very solemn for the news of the queen's imminent
demise had spread as fire spreads through brushwood. The
leader of the deputation spoke 'Your Grace, we have heard the
calamitous news of the queen's approaching death. You are
young yet, your Grace, and may yet beget offspring. We will
send a deputation to the King of Portugal who has a daughter
of child bearing age and who is not yet wed. She is said to be a
fair princess and if you will marry her, your Grace …' 'Stop!'
thundered Richard in a fury 'My wife whom I have loved from
my young years is not dead as yet! How dare you suggest that I
should contemplate any marriage!' His eyes were no longer

blue but dark grey with grief and anger. 'Get you hence all of you, my lords, and do not come again with this cruel suggestion!' he cried out, and then he turned from them visibly shaking. They knew not whether with rage at their suggestion or with grief for his wife.

Never the less, in fear for the kingdom, they began negotiations with Portugal.

Richard crept as close to his wife's new bedchamber as he dared to listen for anything that she might say. There was no sound but her cough which was growing ever weaker, yet the spasms seemed to last longer.

He stood there suffering with her. She, who had been his very life since he was a child, was to leave him without a word of their love said between them. He felt that he could not bear it! He stood there waiting for hours always hoping for the miracle that he so devoutly prayed for.

Someone touched his arm. Richard spun round, his hand on the dagger at his belt. But it was Luke!

'Come, Master Richard' Luke said 'Come away and we will talk.' He took Richard by the arm and led him stumbling away to his own chamber.

This was a strange one now and one that Richard was not yet accustomed to but which was richly furnished. Luke made his master sit on the seat before the fire place where logs were burning. Richard was shaking with cold and misery.

Luke brought wine and food for Richard and made sure that he ate and drank for he had been told that the king had kept a long and fasting vigil. Then he began to talk to his old friend.

No one else could have dared to do this but Luke knew that his words would be well received. 'Master Richard,' he began 'do you recall the night that we rescued Lady Anne from the house called 'The Bird in the Hand?' 'I can never forget it' said

Richard. 'Well, now look you, Master Richard, you have cherished the lady Anne for many years in a truly loving and Christian marriage. Now Master Richard, your wife is called Home.' he said 'We may none of us know when Our Father will send for us, but we do know that one day the call will come.' Richard turned a bleak face to him. 'Luke' he said 'can you do nothing to save my Love?'

The friar shook his head saying 'No, Master Richard, I fear that I cannot. The damp of that dismal place has eaten into her lungs and we cannot revive them' 'So she must die?' Richard's question was as he knew mere rhetoric. 'Yes, Master Richard and cruel would we be to prolong her life in this case.' Luke laid a hand on his friend's shoulder. 'She will be reunited with your son, Master Richard' he said. And then the king broke down and wept openly as Luke held his slender but valiant frame, shaken with sobs, close in his arms.

Luke spoke with one of Anne's physicians and made sure that she had the services of a priest and that she also received a message of love from her husband. The poor lady was so close to death and her breathing so difficult that they could hardly hear her words. Yet they heard one word clearly.

She had asked one of the women who nursed and served her to give a message to the King. She wanted Richard to know that she had loved him for as long as she could remember and had loved no one else.

'Tell him that I will never leave him' she said 'and that one day if God wills it we shall meet again in a better world than this one.'

The next fit of coughing was too great a strain on her sad heart and she slipped into the arms of the Angel of Death murmuring 'My Richard' as her breathing ceased.

Anne died on the sixteenth day of March

'Richard' was the word that was clearly heard..

Queen Anne's funeral was held with great pomp in the Abbey of Westminster where her frail remains were laid by the door to St Edward the Confessor's shrine. King Richard wept openly all the way to the Abbey and throughout the funeral service. When all was done he went to the place where they had laid his wife and stood over her grave weeping bitterly, 'Oh, my Anne! My Lady of Love! How I love you!' he said, and although he knew that her physical ears could no longer hear him yet he hoped that her sweet soul would know how he much loved her and how greatly he grieved her loss.

Luke stayed with his Master Richard for a while and did his best to help him bear the loss of the lady whom he had loved since he was a little boy. But he had to return to his friary, and Richard had still to carry out the duties of a King.

Chapter 41.

A King Alone .

The d King's duties were relentless and now Richard had no sweet companion to talk with when he went to his own rooms in the evening. Richard became more inward looking and sad and yet he worked hard to attempt a new treaty with France.

He was able to make a new treaty with the king of Scotland, in order to defend England's northern borders, and he entertained ambassadors from various countries. Eventually he did make a treaty with France, and he solved the problem of piracy, as well, by his good seamanship, for he went to sea with his fleet. He had been the Lord High Admiral of England since well before the late King Edward had died.

Then somebody started a rumour that Richard wished to marry Elizabeth his brother's oldest daughter. Furious at such a scandalous suggestion Richard called a meeting of all the nobles, politicians, and religious leaders and publicly denounced this rumour as the lie that it was.

He was fond of his niece who was a fair haired and pretty young woman with a gentle and charming manner but his fondness was that of an uncle for his niece it was nothing more. Nor did Richard follow in the footsteps of his brother Edward and take a mistress. He remained in love with his late wife and was determined to be single for as long as he was allowed to do so by his advisors. He named the valiant young Earl of Lincoln as his heir to the throne and refused to contemplate marriage with a princess of any country. He was still mourning his beloved Anne

Not so far off in Brittany Richard's most deadly enemy was planning and plotting with traitors like John Cheney and his ilk, while at home Margaret Beaufort and her husband Lord Stanley and his brother plotted with others who wished to see the end of the Yorkist regime.

Richard had good ears at his disposal and left London to march to Nottingham, his Castle of Care, to await the battle that he knew would come when Henry Tudor managed to make landfall.

King Richard was a skilled commander and had many loyal supporters and well trained and well armed men and great cannons made for him by founders from the Low Countries.

Thus he was ready to do battle with this upstart of a bastard line. He marched his army to Leicester in August. He was ready for a fight and determined to ensure that Tudor would not be successful. Then it became known that Henry Tudor had left his virtual imprisonment in Brittany and had escaped to France by a ruse. Tudor with his French ships and French soldiers landed at Milford Haven on the seventh day of August.

Chapter 42.

The Field of Battle.

King Richard marched to Leicester where he stayed for several
days until he marched his army out of the city to a place called
Redesmere near to the small village of Market Bosworth.

On the twenty second day of August in the year of Our Lord
1485 battle with Tudor and his followers commenced. Richard
had not slept well on the night before and was not as fresh as
he would have wished.

But he had a good array with archers and cannon and a well
tried cavalry.

Further he had never yet lost any battle that he had ever taken
part in. And yet, deep within, he was unsure of himself. He had
lost his son and heir and now his adored Anne was dead. He
had never ceased to grieve for either of them.

A sore heart was no way for a warrior to set out. He ground his
teeth together and tried to summon up the steel in himself. It
was a difficult job, and although he had staunch friends like
Francis Lovell and Jack Howard of Norfolk as well as his
many gentlemen from Yorkshire and most of the nobles of
England around him yet he felt somehow exposed.

He heard Mass and knelt long in prayer. But mostly he found
himself praying for Anne.

He had done whatever he could to keep the children sat Sheriff
Hutton safe and his brother Edward's sons were with them.
The girls were with their mother. Clarence's lad was at Sheriff
Hutton, too. What more could he do? 'I have done all I can, Oh
God, preserve me to rule this fair land of England in a just and

right manner' he prayed. He hoped for an answer from heaven, but of course it did not come.

Just then his Herald, Blanc Sanglier, to inform his that the time had come.

It went well at first for he had chosen a good spot on Ambion Hill and as he trotted forward on White Surrey a great cheer rose from his ranks. He spoke to them, as was the way before a battle, and told them that this fight was for the rightful royal bloodline of England and bade them be courageous. This was much as he always did before a battle. And yet for all the cheers that echoed around him he felt uneasy. There was no Anne to fight for or to go home to afterwards. His advisors had tried to arrange a marriage for him with a Portuguese Princess and that before his beloved Anne, his wife of so many years, was dead! He had been angry but they had told him that he needed an heir, and must think of his kingdom and marry quickly. So he named George of Clarence's lad as his heir. For legitimately so he was. Richard liked the lad, who showed none of his father's bad traits that Richard could see. His own son John of Gloucester was busy on his father's business and was, Richard hoped, well away from the battled field.

King Richard pulled his mind together. These musings were no good on a field of battle! He noted that the two Stanleys, men who served him but whom he mistrusted. Were both drawn up in battle array, but not on the field. They had elected to remained on the edge. He sent a message to Lord Stanley, saying that he, Richard, had with him Stanley's son and heir and that any treachery would result in the lad's death. Stanley sent back a message that he had more sons! This was a clear statement of intent to treason but Richard would not harm Stanley's lad.

However, he knew now that he could not rely on help from that direction. The Stanley family always sat on the fence. Even Anne had told him that.

Battle commenced and all was well with out the help of Lord Stanley. Then Richard saw the impostor, Harry Tudor, being led away, as if from the field. He had a clear path and line of sight to him. He could finish this now! He put spurs to White Surrey and dashed toward the Tudor and his small party. The gigantic form of John Cheney was in his way. To deal with so tall a man, Richard reached down and took hold of his 'morning star' and whorled it round, knocking the giant off his horse and unconscious. The Tudor's standard bearer was his next target, and he went down as well but Richard caught sight of Stanley's men coming onto the field but heading in the wrong direction to serve their king!

Richard saw the trick now and with a mighty cry of 'Treason!' he struck about him as he was surrounded by his enemies. Jack Howard was dead and Lovell he knew was wounded and off the field. He himself was in the thick of his enemies 'Oh God' he prayed 'Let me not be a coward, may I finish this day as King of England and not dishonour my father!' Part of his mind saw Margaret Beaufort's shrewish face. Stanley was her husband and Tudor's step-father, he would not dare go home and say he had fought for King Richard this day! He heard the cries around him 'A Stanley, a Stanley!' and someone pulled him from his saddle. He felt the blows that rained down on him, but fought on, in anger and anguish He heard White Surrey scream. 'Een my horse!' he thought. Then there was a Welsh voice behind him 'Take this for Tudor!' a blow struck his head and the world went black.

Then she was there, before him. Anne! Her golden hair was like a halo round her head. His last breath was the exhalation of her name 'AAAnne!' And then they were together in a beautiful place with no noise of battle but just with sweet music. And he knew that this was heaven Anne took his hand and together they went to meet their son who was also in this beautiful place.

Chapter 43.

Three Days Later.

Friar Luke went to his superior and knelt. 'Father, I have a boon to ask.' 'And what is that, brother Luke?' Luke looked up at his Prior. 'I want permission to take three of my brothers in God and with our wood cart go to the New Work in the town.' Luke said. 'My late Master, King Richard, was good to me and was a patron of this house. His body has lain in the New Work these three days naked with no cover at all to make it decent. It is August, Father, and the flies are busy. Please allow me to bring his body here and bury him in our chapel. Some of my brothers in God are fearful that new king will punish us but I believe he has more on his mind than the dead body of the man whose throne he has usurped.'

The Prior looked sad 'King Richard was indeed a kind patron of our Houses and of many others, too. He was loved by the people who knew him to be just. Go, Luke, take your brethren and your cart and a good sheet. Of course we will bury our late king here in our chapel'.

Thus it was that just before curfew, when all was quiet, four grey friars trundled a hand cart with the wheels wrapped in sacking through the streets of Leicester to the New Work There they tenderly placed the abused body of Richard Plantagenet the last chivalric king of England and the last king of the Yorkist line into the sheet and into their cart. They trundled the cart with its precious cargo back to the Grey Friars.

Going to their chapel which was not large but which was beautiful in its simplicity and a sanctified place, they took up the floor tiles between the choir stalls, before the altar. They dug down into the space where they knew there had many years previously been a burial so that the digging would be easy. And there they made a grave for a king.

When it was dug Luke lifted the bruised and broken body of King Richard the master he had served, the man he had loved as his friend. He had washed the face and the body and made it decent with the sheet, and now he laid it in the grave they had made. He had to squeeze the body in a little for his brethren had dug by eye and not by measure, but he laid Richard down with love, tears steaming down his face. 'Good night, my good Master Richard, may God bless you and have mercy on you! May you be reunited with your beautiful Lady Anne in the hereafter!' he said. And he poured the first handful of earth. The Prior said the service of burial and the monks now in their choir stalls, prayed for their late king. The grave was filled in and the tiles replaced. For there was always the fear that Harry Tudor, as he called himself, might come to look for his prey.

The burial may not have been magnificent as royal burials usually were, but no king was ever laid to rest with more love.

Luke lived long and he was glad when, at last ten years later the new king, styled Henry the Seventh, caused a figure of alabaster to be placed over King Richard's grave with a memorial tablet. Luke did not approve of the words used but at least King Richard was given his titles.

Luke set out on a pilgrimage then. He was going to York and the shrine of Saint William where his master's young wife had gone to pray.

He never returned to the Leicester Grey Friars nor did they ever know where he died or what became of him.

But when in his turn Luke reached the beautiful place, he found himself welcomed by his friend, the generous fellow traveller, his 'Master Richard.'

This book is by its very nature imagination, for we do not know what conversations Richard and Anne and the people around them may have had, although we can guess at the topics they must have discussed.

The author has studied the life and times of King Richard III for sixty years, but does not claim to be an historian, and this book is intended as an historical romance. S.A.C.

10725611R00107

Printed in Great Britain
by Amazon.co.uk, Ltd.,
Marston Gate.